The Hill Billy

Early reviews for
'The Hill Billy'

"There was something magical about growing up in a hill-station in the 1950s. Long walks to school, treks, haunted houses, beauty pageants, leaking roofs, musty cinemas. No traffic jams, no traffic. Days of innocence. Shiv Sharma looks back in affection on his childhood in Mussoorie, his school days, teenage crushes, and the more memorable people who came his way. Good-natured, evoking nostalgia for a forgotten era, this charming memoir is both touching and entertaining. A must read for all those who love the hills."

– Padma Bhushan Ruskin Bond, author of *Room on the Roof,
Our Trees Still Grow in Dehra, A Flight of Pigeons**,
The Blue Umbrella*, *Susanna's Seven Husbands**

"Fluent, natural, light and lively... The opening is powerful and the characters are real... The structure is coherent with the reader longing for more details preferably of the less innocent variety. Everyone loves a success story by the exiled, especially when our mother-in-law's machinations are nullified. It will appeal to the young faced by the trials of growing up, and to the old in recapturing a snatch of post-partition history, no laughing matter for your father's generation which it displaced."

– William (Bill) McKay Aitken, author of
Sri Sathya Sai Baba – A Life, Seven Sacred Rivers and
The Nanda Devi Affair

---

* Made into Hindi movies – *Junoon, The Blue Umbrella* and *7 Khoon Maaf.*

"As early as 1838, the indefatigable traveler Fanny Parks in her diary describes her climb to Mussoorie in a palanquin: *'Such beautiful rhododendrons! They are forest trees, not shrubs, as you have them in England. The people gathered the wild flowers, and filled my lap with them. I could not help sending a man from the plains, who had never seen a nettle, to gather one; he took hold of it, and relinquishing his hold instantly in excessive surprise, exclaimed, 'It has stung me; it is a scorpion plant!'*

"And Shiv Sharma's *The Hill Billy* has his own bouquet of stinging nettles where the Himalayan foothills come alive in a fast paced, scintillating account of growing up in the fast-fading hill resort of Mussoorie in the 1950-60s. This entertaining tour d'horizon begins where the Raj and its minions had already packed their bags and gone, leaving behind a legacy of missionary schools, hand-pulled rickshaws, fancy fairs and picnic hampers. A spicy survey of a hill-stations, past and present, is packed with lively anecdotes about its people, eccentrics, characters, scandals – everything that makes the place unique.

"There's never a dull moment in this fascinating chronicle of the hills to the north."

> – Ganesh Saili, author of *Mussoorie Medley. Himalaya* and the upcoming *Gupp and Gossip – From the Hills*

The Hill Billy

Shivdutt Sharma

INDIA
IMPRESSIONS

**INDIA
IMPRESSIONS**
THE HILL BILLY
First published in India in 2014 by
India Impressions
(A Division of Yogi Impressions Books Pvt. Ltd.)
1711, Centre 1, World Trade Centre,
Cuffe Parade, Mumbai 400 005, India.
Website: www.indiaimpressions.com

First Edition, March 2014

Cover design by: Priya Mehta

The names of certain characters, living or dead, and places
in this novel have been changed to protect their identities.
Any resemblance to a person living or dead is therefore purely
coincidental and unintended.

ISBN 978-81-926896-0-9

Printed at: Repro India Ltd., Mumbai

So I've been told...

Prologue

Angry.

Turbulent.

Vicious.

Violent.

The river that normally ran shallow and placid had overnight swollen in the July rain to a flood.

The small bus carrying sixteen people including mine and our neighbour's family, both fleeing from Sialkot in Pakistan, came to a halt at the riverbank. The driver turned and asked my father, "*Ab kya karna hai Bauji?*"[1]

"*Paar toh jaana hi hai, Makhan Singh...*"[2]

"*Toh Bauji, bacchon ko bus mein baitha rehne doh, aur aap sab badhey log uttar kar paidal chalo nahin toh paar jaana namumkin hai.*"[3]

Drenched to the bone, families formed a human chain to

---

1 What should we do now, Sir?

2 We have to cross the river somehow, Makhan Singh.

3 Then Sir, let the children remain in the bus but the elders must get off and cross on foot. Otherwise, we won't be able to make the crossing.

cross over to the opposite bank. Men unrolled their *saafaas*[4] and women removed their *dupattas*[5] to bind each other around the waists so no one would get swept away in the gushing, swirling waters. It was a precarious crossing. Several men had children hoisted on their backs or across their shoulders. Wailing babes-in-arms clutched tightly to their mothers' breasts.

My eldest sister, Raj, who was around six-years-old then, recalls that when the bus reached midway in the river, it suddenly stalled and began to float. Terrified, the driver shouted to the people to put their shoulders to it and push with all their might. Panic-stricken by the screams of the children trapped in the bus, they pushed with all their strength and as luck would have it, the bus coughed to a start. Makhan Singh pumped the clutch pedal and slammed the accelerator.

The rhythmic chant of "*Chalte raho! Badhte raho!*"[6] kept the human chain ploughing doggedly through the waist-high waters. Relentlessly, rain poured down on their heads. In the mêlée some panic-stricken mothers, in a desperate bid to save their own lives, plucked the burden of newborn babies from their chests and flung them into the raging flood waters. Others hardened their hearts and deliberately let go of the hands of older relatives to be engulfed by the strong current, so they could cross over to safety.

It wasn't just a country that had been sundered. Families had been riven apart in the aftermath of the partition of India.

---

[4] Turbans.

[5] A kind of stole worn by women, draped across the shoulders.

[6] Keep moving! Keep going forward!

Chapter 1

Fruit of the Womb

I was born of a mango.

And that's not as absurd as it sounds. For this was no ordinary mango.

The thing is that my mother had already given birth to two daughters before and now that she was with child again for the third time, my grandmother, who was not going to put up with the wails of a third girl child, had decided to take the matter into her own firm hands. Her friends had told her about a sadhu who had just returned from the Himalayas to his ashram on the outskirts of our town and who was renowned for granting the boon of a male child to a pregnant woman. So, the next morning she instructed my mother to put on her red brocade sari and gold jewellery and, without informing the men folk, called for the family's tonga[1], and both the women rode off to visit the sadhu baba.

Reaching there, my grandmother immediately bossed her way in, ahead of the other women who had come on similar missions, and prostrated before the baba declaring she would not get up until he blessed her daughter-in-law with a male

---

[1] A two-wheeled, horse-drawn carriage.

child. Under no condition did she want another girl born in her house this time! Imperious, even in her request that came across as a demand, she got up, adjusted the *pallu*² over her head, and pushed my mother forward saying, 'Give her something, babaji, so the child in her womb will definitely be a male child!'

Now, as my mother later told me, the sadhu baba put his hand behind his back and pulled out a ripe, golden mango from a basket. He muttered something and blew on the mango... "*Phhoo-ooo!*" He then asked her to hold out her pallu, like one would while begging for alms, and dropping the mango into it said, "*Ja suputri, iss baar tere yahan ladka hi paida hoga...*"³ Having got the desired blessing, both the women then walked out and down the path from the ashram. As my mother was passing by the tamarind trees that grew along the path, a bunch of sour-sweet tamarinds fell at her feet. She quickly bent to scoop them up, without my grandmother noticing her, and hid them in the folds of her pallu. Reaching home, she washed and dried them and enjoyed sucking the brown flesh off the seeds in the privacy of her bedroom.

On the ride back home in the tonga, my grandmother saw to it that my mother squeezed the juice and pulp out of the ripe mango and sucked it right down to the *guthli*⁴ which she told her to wrap in her handkerchief and plant it in the garden when they got home. "...and, see that you water it and pray before it every day, first thing after taking your bath," her tone, which was unusually tart, was surprisingly tender and full of concern at that moment. My mother, who usually never had a good word to say about her mother-in-law, later confessed that she felt a surge of respect for the older woman then.

---

² The loose end of the sari.
³ Go daughter, this time you will give birth to a son.
⁴ Seed.

That is how, seven or eight months later, I came into the world – via a mango.

Around 1.30 am (the clocks had been advanced by an hour during wartime), the midwife rushed out of my mother's room to excitedly announce, "*Mataji, mataji beta hua hai!*"[5] I believe that is one of the rare occasions that my grandmother's face lit up as an electric bulb. She hugged her son who was pacing the corridor outside the room and blessed him, "At last, someone to carry forward the family name... now let me go in and check if all his limbs are intact... and you, wake up the servant. Tell them to turn on all the lights in the house... and call for the tonga, now!"

"Mitto," she instructed her thirteen-year-old daughter, "Go and light the diya in the puja room and ring the bell to let Krishnaji[6] know, that a son is born to my son!"

"*Bebe*[7]," reasoned my father, "Why do you want a tonga now... where do you want to go at this hour of the night?"

"Uufffff-ho, Parkaa-aash[8]," she turned to him, "I'm not going anywhere but I've been waiting for four years now for this event, so I can proudly tell my brothers in the village that a grandson is born in our house. Go, tell Rashid to ride out now to Ugoki[9] and break the good news! I cannot wait till the morning! And then go in and see the face of your son!"

And that's how the news travelled from Ghent to Aix, or in this case, from Sialkot to Ugoki[10] some fifty-odd miles away from each other.

---

5 Mataji, Mataji... a son is born.
6 A reference to Lord Krishna.
7 A term of endearment used for a mother or grandmother in Punjabi.
8 That happens to be my father's first name.
9 The name of our ancestral village.
10 Two hamlets in the north-east of the Punjab province of Pakistan.

My mother recalls that when she heard she had delivered a boy, she fainted out of sheer mental exhaustion and relief and slept for a good fourteen hours, something that the barbs and taunts of her mother-in-law had deprived her of, over the years. Constantly living under the fear of a possible second marriage of her husband, if she did not produce a male child, she had tremulously borne her third pregnancy. "Thank God, that mango did the trick," she would declare with a deep sigh of relief whenever she got into a reminiscent mood.

Naturally, she continued to relish mangoes for the rest of her life. Mangoes in pickle, mango pulp in milkshake, mango slices in curd, mango lassi, mango aam-papad, mango chutney, mango *barfi*[11], mango ice cream... you could think of any number of creative ways to consume mangoes, yet she could surprise you with a new preparation. During the mango season, she would polish off three or four mangoes at a time – even when they started costing Rs.500 a dozen!

Of course, since these were not bewitched but ordinary mangoes, there was no fear of causing any unwanted pregnancy!

---

[11] A popular Indian sweetmeat.

Chapter 2

The Din and the Djinn

The village had come to the town.

Bebeji, my grandmother, who was at last able to push her chest out and hold her head high now that she had a grandson to carry forward the family name, had invited all her relatives, far and near, dear and not so dear, from Ugoki for my *mundan*[1]. Till the age of four, my hair had not seen the scissor and had been allowed to grow. I'm told it was braided into seven or eight plaits that would now be chopped off at this grand ceremony that every male child in the Punjabi community has to undergo.

In an effort to appease my mother's parents, whom she had in no uncertain ways made feel unwelcome on the birth of my two elder sisters, Bebeji displayed rare largesse of heart by inviting not just my mother's parents this time but also her brother and his family, plus her sister and husband for the gala event.

The guests started arriving a week before the mundan was to take place. Tents had been pitched in the spacious grounds across the three houses that belonged to us, to accommodate outstation guests from the extended families of either side. The horse was in a sweat for that whole week carting the folks who arrived

---

[1] A head-shaving ritual of male children, followed by Hindus.

by bus or train. Rashid, who drove the tonga, swore under his breath at a bunch of uncouth villagers he had to transport in the tonga that he thought was no less than a plush Victoria carriage, fit only to ferry his aristocratic masters. However, since he too could not contain his joy at the arrival of the son his *Bauji*[2] had fathered, he put up a brave face during his long duty hours and the innumerable rides to and fro.

The house resounded with the din and clamour of the guests. Space had been cordoned off for the *halwais*[3] hired to prepare special meals for the guests – breakfast, lunch, teatime treats and dinner – during their stay. A place of honour had been reserved in the new house for Swamiji, who had arrived with a dozen of his disciples from Haridwar. Their quarters reeked with the smell of *ghee*[4], milk, stale flowers, sweat and *dhoop*[5] smelling of roses, jasmine and sandalwood. My father's elder uncle, Kharaiti Lal, had been given a private room on the first floor as he was a known tippler and meat eater. Outwardly adopting a gracious air towards Swamiji, Kharaiti Lal had however brought his own objects of worship: a framed photo of *Kali*,[6] a small *Shivalinga*[7] and an icon of *Bhairon*[8].

Almost everyone in the family would get petrified when Uncle Kharaiti Lal came for a visit. Even his sister, my grandmother, who usually walked roughshod over everyone, was wary of him when he was in the vicinity. Since Uncle appeared to be rather fond of my mother, my grandmother would try, at least in his presence, to hold back her venomous

---

[2] Master.

[3] Cooks, who specialise in making Indian sweetmeats.

[4] Clarified butter.

[5] Fragrant incense sticks burnt during prayer sessions.

[6] The goddess of death and destruction worshipped fervently in West Bengal.

[7] Representation of the union of male and female principles symbolising Creation.

[8] A demi-god appeased with the offering of meat and liquor.

tongue that she would otherwise spray regularly on my mother. However, this being a time of festivity and celebrations, everyone was in a happy and jovial mood.

In addition to the people camping in the house, a regular stream of guests from the neighbouring mohallas[9], also kept pouring in throughout the day. Work in my father's sports goods manufacturing factory had almost come to a standstill because the workforce had been roped in to look after the guests and service their needs. Some of them had been deputed to distribute invitation cards for the mundan ceremony to my father's business associates, namely, bankers, suppliers and friends.

Unknown to anyone in the family and drowned out by the band-baaja[10] and din of the celebrations, a fleeting rumour about the outbreak of haija[11] in a distant mohalla, had gone unreported in the house. So when Uncle Kharaiti Lal didn't come down from his room at dinner time, citing stomach upset, no one saw it as a cause for alarm. For one, he was getting on in age and had been feeling rather drained out with the stress of the celebrations. Still, concerned, my father went up the stairs to check on him after dinner and found the door locked from inside. Yelling, "Chachaji, Chachaji, tussi theek ho na?"[12] he got a grunt in reply "Aaho!"[13] Satisfied with that response, my father came down the stairs and disappeared into his bedroom. Everyone retired early that night, for the next morning, the mundan was to start at around ten.

That winter in Sialkot was bitterly cold, so most guests were sleeping snugly under heavy quilts. My mother recalls that she was too tired to even go to sleep that night and was

---

9 Zones.
10 Music instruments.
11 Cholera, a dreaded water-borne disease.
12 Uncle, Uncle... Are you alright?
13 Yes!

lying half awake next to my father in the bedroom, with her mind mulling over the details of the next day's ceremony. She suddenly heard a violent fit of coughing, followed by a loud groan of 'Hhaa-aai...'[14] and the crash of a glass bottle. Frightened out of her wits, she shook my father awake and asked him to quickly go up and check on Chachaji because she had heard him groaning in pain. He ran up the stairs, and to his surprise found the door ajar, as if someone had just entered or exited the room. On entering, he found Chachaji sprawled half off the bed, his eyes wide open and splinters of glass strewn across the floor. Chachaji had chosen a rather unfortunate time to die. The doctor said the cholera took him. My grandmother said it was the booze. And my mother said it was one of Bhairon's Djinns[15] whom Chachaji had kept captive in a bottle with the power of his *siddhi*[16] that had finally escaped its bottle-prison with the last groan from Chachaji.

Whatever it was, it cast a pall of gloom over the function, the next day. The band-baaja got silenced. The lavish feast was cancelled. Swamiji however announced that despite the death in the family, the mundan would be performed, as scheduled. I'm told, I bawled throughout the head-shave and got a few nicks from the barber's sharp razor that glinted menacingly in his hand. He was instructed to get the job done without the least bit fuss or bother. Swamiji whispered my birth name in my ear and left, soon after, saying it was not good for him to stay on in a house of death.

Every one or two years, my sisters and I sit to reminisce the past. My eldest sister, who has now taken over from my dear departed mother, begins to roll out the family skeletons one by one and give them a good airing before they are shunted

---

[14] A Hindi expression for "Oh!"

[15] Minions.

[16] Spiritual powers, sometimes Tantric, to control a spirit and make it do one's bidding.

back into the closet. She never fails to regale us and, at the same time, send a cold shiver down our spines as she relives the events of the mundan ceremony with us. At the end of the tale, she pauses to catch her breath, and looking directly at me, she has the habit of shaking her head and lamenting, "Ohhh... no wonder you are always so pissed off with everyone and don't care for us, nor call us often. Somewhere, you still hold a grouse at having your gala mundan ceremony ruined by that old Bhairon-*bhakt*[17]!"

---

[17] Worshipper.

Chapter 3

Death at Prayer

Shouts and loud cries rent the air of a peaceful evening. A train thundered by, on the tracks just below the railway quarters where we had sought refuge, after fleeing Sialkot, with our paternal uncle who lived in Tees Hazari in old Delhi. Our tea-time togetherness had just been blasted by the special news bulletin on the radio that had a minute ago been blaring a Hindi film song. Pandemonium broke out as we all rushed into the compound.

"*Hai Ram, goli maar di aarati de waqt.*"[1]

"*Someone has shot the Mahatma!*"

"*Ai ki ho gaya!*"[2]

What were they yelling about? Why was my father suddenly pulling on his *achkan*[3], and looking for his walking stick? Why was Bebeji beating her breasts? I was utterly confused.

"*Tussi kitthay ja rahe ho jee?*"[4] asked my mother, clutching my father by his arm.

---

[1] Hey Ram, someone shot him at the time of prayer.
[2] Oh God, why has this happened!
[3] A long, knee-length, body-fitting coat.
[4] Where are you going?

"*Lai, saari dilli Birla Mandir wal paj rayee veh, mein vi othay ja raya waah,*"[5] he said in a small, panicked voice.

Mahatma Gandhi, after emerging from his evening prayer to meet the crowds gathered outside, had just been shot on the premises of Birla Mandir in Delhi.

"*Parkaa-aash, mein vi tere nal chalni aaa,*"[6] shrieked Bebeji pulling her soiled, white dupatta over her head.

Of course, after the initial clamour and confusion had died down, no one was willing to venture out of the house. Soon, a kind of an eerie quiet descended with the darkness on the railway colony.

A few days later, the recording company HMV brought out a 78 rpm, two-disc song by Mohammed Rafi on the life and death of Mahatma Gandhi. "*Suno, suno ai duniywaalo, Bapu ki yeh amar kahani...*"[7] began the mournful and soulful voice of Rafi. And guess who rushed out to buy the first few copies before they could sell out faster than hot *jalebis*[8]? My father of course, who wouldn't stop playing the records over and over again on his cousin's wind-up gramophone! Tears would well up in his eyes and flow down his cheeks that he would keep dabbing at with his white handkerchief plucked from the side-pocket of his starched *kurta*[9]. Any wonder, I remember snatches of its lyrics to this day?!

Such was my introduction to Delhi, of which I carry only fleeting images and impressions...

... being jostled and pushed around, perched on my uncle's shoulders to catch a glimpse of the flower-laden truck that seemed

---

5 All of Delhi will be rushing towards Birla Mandir, even I'm going there!

6 Prakash (her son), even I am coming with you.

7 Listen, listen, all you people of this world, to Bapu's immortal story...

8 A popular Indian sweetmeat, served at breakfast time.

9 A loose, long shirt worn by men in north Indian villages.

to be followed by millions of people lining the funeral route.

... hiding indoors in the cramped two room railway quarter for almost a week, because I had uttered supposedly vile abuse at one of the older boys, who lived a few quarters away, and who had threatened to beat me to pulp the next time he saw me around. This bears some telling, as the memory of it still makes me laugh...

What happened was this: One sultry May afternoon, we were playing *gulli-danda*[10]. A boy, older to me, who lived next door – I think his name was Razdan – accidentally tripped me over. I must have grazed my elbows or shins, but I do recall I yelled out *"Madarchod"*[11] and threatened that I would get my father to shoot him! Then I ran inside the green-fenced compound and quickly latched the gate. Razdan came to the window, banged his fist on it and shouted words to the effect "Come out, you little twerp... I'll pull your tongue out!" I scuttled under the bed so he couldn't spot me, even if the window was to fly open with his persistent banging.

I didn't step out of the house for almost a week! Everyone wondered what was wrong and started nagging me, but I didn't venture beyond the safety of the green fence. After a few days, one of my older friends called Parveen, who lived a few cottages away, came to enquire if I was sick and I blubbered the real reason. He laughed and laughed... and just wouldn't stop. Then he said, *"Achha*[12], you come with me tomorrow to his house and we will settle the matter." I quipped, "Why should I go to him, he is nothing but a low-down boy?" But he said that since I was the one who was cowering and running shit-scared of him, I should come along and apologise. He said,

---

[10] An Indian game played on the streets with one long wooden stick and a smaller, double-pointed wooden bar.

[11] Mother-fucker.

[12] Okay.

"See, then you will be able to come out of the house and visit me every evening like you used to before!"

So without telling anyone in the family what had happened, I went to Parveen's house. He offered me a cup of tea and some *namkeens*[13] and coached me on what to say. Then we went over to Razdan's place. That good-looking snoot was sleeping like a maharaja at five in the evening, but his mother offered to wake him up. Hair tousled, wearing crumpled pyjamas, and scratching his crotch, he came out rubbing the sleep out of his eyes that popped open like window shutters when he saw me sitting there clicking my boots. He muttered, "Hello!" to Parveen, while pointedly ignoring me. So Parveen brought up the subject. I mumbled an apology and we both were made to shake hands.

What a relief!! At last, I was free to show my face again in the compound and roam around without the fear of Razdan ruining my happiness. Actually, he then went on to become quite friendly with me. He even condescended to take me on his team when the boys gathered to play volleyball. I was naturally thrilled. I had secretly admired his looks and his lanky physique, ever since their family had arrived from Pakistan, two months ago.

I have always maintained that I don't remember much of my childhood. Yet, it's rather surprising how, when one seriously thinks about it, some long-buried memories from the past start stirring and then, without a warning, rise and flow over like tea boiling over the pot it's being brewed in!

I recall that the uncle whose house we were staying in had a rather long-nosed daughter who must have been around nine or ten at that time. Her hair was always oiled and tightly pulled away on either side with a centre parting that appeared like

---

13 Savoury tea-time snacks.

a clear road on her head, and twisted and turned into a plait that was tied with a bright-coloured ribbon. Bimla, as she was called, would grudgingly go to school every morning, while we would sleep late and play all day. She couldn't wait to rush home from school to join in our games. Even at that age, she had a voice that sounded like the braying of a donkey. Poor, plain-Jane Bimla. (It took ages, and unceasing efforts on the part of her parents to get her married off.) However, she could keep us in splits with her jokes and pranks. We had great fun with her. At last, after braving three months of Delhi's sweltering summer, by which time all of us from cooler climes had wilted sufficiently, came the day when we had to bid adieu to Delhi. My dad hired a tan-and-brown Buick Station Wagon to cart us to a hill station that was eight hours away by road. A fortnight earlier he along with his personal assistant had gone there to rent a bungalow and stock it with supplies that would last us during our long stay. That particular morning, we got packed into the back seats of the Station Wagon – a grumpy grandmother, a snivelling aunt, four children and two parents in the front seat with the driver. Prem and Babu, our domestic helps, were huddled into the dickey with its door kept ajar for the journey. I don't much remember about the rest of the journey, but I wouldn't be surprised if I were told that *Dilliwalas*[14] were only too relieved to see us depart and finally have some peace in their houses. Ah, the dilemma of relatives... they can't really turn their backs on refugees who land up at their doorstep unannounced, can they?

---

[14] Residents of Delhi.

And so it came to pass...

Chapter 4

The Hills of Mansuri

Veils of mist drifted down the hills as our old Station Wagon coughed and drew to a halt at a teashop sitting precariously on a sharp bend. I hopped out of the car with Prem. Three-fourth of the teashop appeared to be hanging in mid-air with a discernible backward tilt to its floor that suggested it might just tip over and fall into the ravine below. A rumble of thunder echoed and rolled across the sky, as dark grey clouds hovered menacingly over the mountaintops. A cold chill ran up my wet, cotton-shirted back as I hurried back into the Wagon to get squashed between my sisters. The teashop *bhula*[1] promptly served us smudgy glasses of piping hot tea.

Prem came clutching a bunch of bluish ticket stubs in his fist. "*Bauji,*" he addressed my father, "*Chalo, toll tax par ditta vey.*"[2] My aunt, who had been retching and puking non-stop as the Station Wagon had begun winding its way up the cork-screw road, was reluctantly pushed, whining and complaining, into the back seat and given a slice of lemon dipped in salt to suck. My mother, who was made of sturdier stuff, and had apparently been impervious to the stomach-churning effects of the zigzag turns,

---

[1] A young boy.
[2] Sir, let's go, I have paid the toll tax.

16

curled her lips into a sneer and cast a withering look in the direction of my aunt, but it was totally lost on her as she had her eyes screwed up tight. However, Bebeji caught my mother's look and sneer, and sent an ominous scowl her way. With a rattle and a roll, the old warhorse heaved on its wheels and began a slow, laborious climb, up the mist-shrouded mountainside.

Suddenly, a large drop of water plopped and splattered across the Wagon's windshield. "Quick, roll up the windows!" ordered my mother as more fat drops fell before torrential rain began to lash at our four-wheeled warhorse. With a groan, it shuddered to a stop on the next curve. Now what! Prem, his brother Babu and my father got out, and putting their hands and shoulders to the Wagon's rump heaved and pushed with all their might. Instead of moving forward, it rolled back and we all screamed with fright. A few *coolies*[3] who had taken shelter from the downpour by an overhanging rock quickly came to put some big stones behind the rear wheels and pitched in to lend their muscle and might to the sliding Wagon. It inched forward, grunted, coughed and got moving again. The coolies cheered and ran after the vehicle with their palms outstretched, jostling one another for *baksheesh*[4] for their labours.

At the end of the climb, the road suddenly flattened out and the last lap of the drive was a breeze. Up another short, rocky climb and the Station Wagon came to a halt at a curve in front of a broken wooden gate. A gravelled slope ran down a couple of yards towards a white-and-green bungalow standing amid Apricot, *Peepul*[5] and Oak trees on an acre of land.

The rain hadn't stopped. Hurrying up the slope towards us was the *chowkidar*[6], clutching a couple of umbrellas under his

---

3 Luggage bearers.
4 A small monetary tip.
5 A Ficus or Ashwatha tree is of great importance in India and known to cure several diseases.
6 Caretaker.

arms. My sisters and I ran down the slope to take shelter under a covered porch. Bebeji and our aunt, whom we addressed as *Buaji*[7], followed us, treading rather inelegantly on the gravel. The chowkidar had made the beds and piled them with heavy quilts. These had been bought by my father with his former business associate, Mulkh Raj, on their previous trip to the house. The suited-booted, toothbrush-moustached Mulkh Raj had stayed behind to air out and stock up the house, while father returned to Delhi to fetch his family.

We were quickly hustled to the bedrooms. I was yelling, '*Peshaab aaya, peshaab aaya*'[8] and hopping on my feet. Halfway down, not being able to hold the water back any longer, I let loose a stream of piss right on the *dhurried*[9] wooden floor. Thus was the house anointed by the youngest male member of the Sharma family.

Pretty soon, Bishna, the chowkidar, came up the creaking wooden staircase, bearing a tray with a large pot of steaming hot tea and crisp biscuits. Someone poured it into pre-warmed cups and handed it to us. Worn out from the long drive from Delhi, we dozed off and went to sleep.

That's how we found ourselves, eight months after our flight from Pakistan, ensconced in a damp-smelling bungalow at the highly Anglicised hill station of Mussoorie – a name derived from the native, purple-coloured berry shrub called Mansur that is the staple fodder for mountain goats that graze the hills. The hill folk however call it Mansuri. From a small hunting box constructed in 1820 along one of the back roads by one Mr. Shore, a Joint Magistrate of Revenues in Dehradun, Mansuri began to flourish as a hill resort under Captain Young of the Royal Engineers. As the Commandant of Landour, a small

---

[7] Maternal aunt.
[8] I have to piss.
[9] Carpeted.

hamlet at the north-eastern tip of Mussoorie, which he developed as a Military Cantonment, Captain Young built his sprawling mansion christened Mullingar, on a promontory overlooking the Doon valley. The hilly area south of Landour later grew into a civilian township.

Our house sat quietly hidden in the thick of a forest at the extreme end of the town in what was called the 'Happy Valley'. A poorly-tarred road wound its way along solitary hills, kissed only fleetingly by the sun. Just before the tar path gave way to a mud road, a slope branched off and ran sharply up a hillside. One had to lure the *rickshawallas*[10] with an extra rupee or two to pull the rickshaw up the steep climb. Mostly, however, we just left them on the road and footed it up, past a few houses that remained deserted for the better part of the year.

Dil Bahar, or 'seasons of the heart', was once the private residence of one of the *begums*[11] of the Nawab of Rampur, a princely state in eastern Uttar Pradesh, famous for its Rampuri *chakkoos*[12] that were used for various nefarious and sometimes murderous purposes. This stone-and-wood, one-storey bungalow, with four servants' quarters (which in today's inflationary times are referred to politely as outhouses and have been bought out and renovated by the nouveau riche of Punjab and Delhi), was just ideal for our family of eight and four servants, three of whom had worked for my father in Sialkot and had thrown in their lot with him by accompanying the family to the hills.

We settled in quite fast. There hadn't been much to unpack, for hadn't I heard that we had slipped out of Pakistan with just the clothes on our backs, and not much else?

Dil Bahar...

---

10 Pullers of a two wheeled carriage.
11 Wives.
12 Knives.

Just muttering that name, even after forty-odd years, makes my heart beat faster and my eyes sparkle with joy. The slope that led down to it had four rows of terraced fields along one side where nothing grew except a lone, stunted apple tree that hadn't borne fruit for years. At times, instead of coming down the slope, I would hop from field to field in the direction of the house. The uppermost field had a strange tree, I can't remember its name now, that would swing and sway dangerously when we pushed it on our return from school. Why I gave it a couple of shoves every day, I don't have the faintest idea. Perhaps it was in the hope of seeing it getting uprooted and toppling over to block the path to the house. But that swinging tree never did oblige and stands tall to this day, while I've grown old and am ready to topple over myself. The lowest field had a sturdy apricot tree that bore the juiciest, orange-coloured apricots in summer. It was on the branch of this tree that the servants looped two ropes over and put a large oaken plank for us to swing on. Below it ran a narrow, open drain that was mostly dry. Every time the swing swung over it, we would place bets on who could spit right into the drain.

The front and rear of Dil Bahar had two green-painted, hexagonal, glass-paned projections that were the only bit of design inputs for the big, boxy house. One abutted from the dining room, while the other abutted from the drawing room[13] in the rear end of the house. Two high-stepped, concrete staircases ran oddly on either side of the front. One led to a bathroom and the other to a small dressing room. A wooden stairway at the rear end ran up to the puja room. The grounds at the front and rear were scattered with gravel, a typical feature of the houses in Mussoorie[14].

For some odd reason, the ground at the back was at a raised level and one had to climb up three steps to get there.

---

13 A living room.
14 The modern name of the Hill Station.

Equally strange, it was called the 'kirkit' ground, perhaps slang for 'cricket'. Maybe the erstwhile Nawab played cricket with his begums there – who knows? But for all our Anglicised, missionary upbringing we continued to call it the 'kirkit' ground. Initially, it served as our playing field for games like 'Highland-Lowland', hopscotch etc. It also served as a drying field with clotheslines running from end to end. Below the ground grew a lone rhododendron tree among several oak trees. It bore large crimson flowers that, besides their opulent beauty, also made for a deliciously sour rhododendron chutney spiked with onions and red chillies.

Over the next two years, creeper vines that my mother planted would flower with pink, lilac and yellow Dutch roses and Primroses that came to cover the front and back walls of Dil Bahar.

Like the four ventricles of the heart chamber, four suites occupied the top floor with each suite comprised of one large bedroom, a dressing room, a storeroom and an attached bathroom. At the ground level, there was a drawing room on one side and a fairly huge dining room with a table to seat twenty-four people, on the other. Attached to them were subsidiary rooms with attached toilets. One of these rooms served as my father's office-cum-shaving room complete with a dresser and an office table on which his 1940s portable Remington typewriter sat. The room opposite it served as my bedroom when I became old enough to sleep alone.

The entrance to the house was through an ample porch covered by a sloping tin roof placed over slightly rotting poles and wooden beams. A green wooden fence ran in an L-shape around the kirkit ground and along the side of the house, right up to the kitchen. This was adorned by creeper vines blooming with the exotic whitish-green, purple-coloured Passion flowers. During the day, we would usually sit out here and laze around. This was also the portion of the house where the family would entertain visitors who casually dropped by.

One afternoon, my father, my youngest sister Tuti and I were sitting there playing with one of our dogs, Bingo. Suddenly, without warning, one of the poles emitted a sharp, pistol-like crack and the roof came down on us. With a terrified yelp, the dog leapt out. My father who was sitting half in and half out of the porch simply tilted back in his chair and fell out on the ground. I managed to also get out rather quickly but Tuti, like a pigeon, had shut her eyes and stayed put hunched over in a foetal position. "Where's Tuti... where's Tuti... hasn't she got out?" screamed my mother. "*Mein aiday haithaan vaan, paboji,*"[15] Tuti trilled from under the collapsed roof. She stuck an arm and a leg out through the beams and was pulled out unhurt. The entrance to the house wore a rather denuded look without that porch for over a year, until my father decided to prop it up once again.

We all blossomed and flowered while we were at Dil Bahar.

---

[15] I am under here, 'Paboji' – a term we addressed our mother by. And there's a story in that as well. As is common in most Indian families, my mother and grandmother (that's her mother-in-law) never got along. To spite her, my mother trained us to call our grandmother 'Bebeji' which really means an old crone, while our grandmother was still probably in her late-thirties. To get back at her, our grandmother told us not to address our mother as 'Ma' or the increasingly popular 'Mummy' but to call her 'Paboji' – a word that usually conjures up an image of a fat, dumpy woman. When I heard this story, years later from my mother – I was in my forties then – I laughed and laughed... and so did she.

Chapter 5

A Crooked Board on a Bent Pole

The narrow, wooden board hung crookedly, strung by a wire twisted around an electric pole whose angle continued to tilt like that of the Leaning Tower of Pisa. Painted in black and white, it bore 'O. P. Sharma of Sialkot' proclaiming the new occupant of Dil Bahar. For some odd reason, the 'of Sialkot' was written in italics. The 'O. P.' was unnecessary and served only as an identification to the postman because the rest of the town referred to my father as '*Panditji*[1]' or 'Sharmaji'. The 'of Sialkot' tag I think was nostalgic of his recent exodus from Pakistan and of the three houses and business that he had left behind. Otherwise, who in this remote Himalayan hill station could have heard of, or have been bothered about Sialkot?

It was also strange that the hill folk and the *baniya*[2] shopkeepers should address him as Panditji because he never dressed like a Hindu and always wore an achkan over his white *salwar* – the traditional attire of the Muslim gentry of Pakistan and, more particularly, the Pathans of Peshawar[3]. His feet were always encased in the upturned, elaborately embroidered, nawabi

---

[1] A respected form of addressing a Hindu brahmin.

[2] A community of shopkeepers.

[3] An erstwhile tribal, underdeveloped district of undivided Pakistan.

footwear. Indeed, his name, Om Prakash Sharma, was totally at odds with his sartorial style. Six feet tall, dark and handsome with natural waves in his hair, always held in place with the red Swastik Hair Oil, and lean as a pine tree, my father always walked with a cane that he swung in an elegant manner in his right hand. He had quite an impressive collection of canes.

My mother was quite the opposite. Naturally fair as the Pathani women, if not fairer, she went a step further and emerged as the fairest of them all with a liberal dusting of Max Factor face powder. Where he was lean, she was fat, although I would rather use the word buxom. But then, she really did have a broad beam and a thick waist. However her beauty overshadowed her lack of height. The height she would compensate for by sporting slender, high-heeled sandals. She must have perfected the balancing act on them for never once did she twist her ankle or sprain a leg, while going up and down the steep slopes of Mussoorie. While the Anglo-Indian ladies strapped their bosoms and covered them with neck-high frilled blouses, my mother's necklines plunged to showcase her fair cleavage which I'm positive also received its share of pats from the powder puff. This was always a sore point with my grandmother and my aunt, who by the way, was flat as a board. The more they frowned on her necklines, the deeper she made them plunge.

Bebeji, about whom you may have by now formed some kind of an opinion, was the matriarch. She wore a salwar and kurta, usually thick woollen ones in earth tones of grey, green and brown, paired with a white *mulmul*[4] dupatta. She wore no jewellery. Her only adornments were the deep creases and frown lines that appeared on her forehead and the rest of her face. She was nut brown and, come hail or shine, always went around barefoot. The soles of her feet must have been thicker than that of a camel's. I never heard her raise her voice at anyone.

---

[4] A light, voile-like fabric.

She conveyed what she had to through grumbling and muttering in stage whispers into the ears of her son, her daughter and the servants... making sure her voice carried to my mother's diamond-studded ears.

Mitto, her daughter's (my aunt's) pet name was nowhere close to Savitri, which was her rather sanctimonious real name. She was a graduate and she could read the English language newspaper. That's why she was deputed to help us in our homework and get us off to school in the mornings. She also dressed in the style of our grandmother, except that she wore floral-printed satin and silk *salwar-kameez*[5] suits in pastel hues. She also wore *chappals*[6] on her feet, and scorned the high heels that my mother wore. She was a tall woman with a nose as patrician as my father's and would keep biting her nails while she devoured a battery of newspapers and magazines. She also had the rather peculiar habit of wiping her body clean with swabs of cotton wool soaked in denatured spirit after a regular bath with soap and water. An asthmatic from a young age, she would keep everyone awake into the middle of the night with her non-stop bouts of coughing and wheezing. These stopped miraculously after she got married. But, more on Savitri in a later chapter.

Raj, the first-born of my parents, whose actual name was Rajkumari, which literally translated means a princess, was the apple of our father's eye. Typically, in Indian families, the eldest and the youngest child are loved more than the ones who come in between. Raj was also the cleverest among us, always securing a first or second rank in her class. I don't recall her interacting much with us while we were growing up, as she was a few years elder to us. She took after our mother in height and structure. Oh, my father was so proud of her when she passed her Junior Cambridge exam in second division and then, two years later, her Senior Cambridge with the same rank.

---

5 A garment usually worn by Punjabi women.

6 Flip-flops.

He lovingly called her 'Munni' and was the only one to do so. To the rest of us, she was Raj. When she left Mussoorie to join Sophia College in Bombay, my father was inconsolable and could be seen shedding copious tears whenever she called, or he spoke to her on the phone. Her visits home during vacations were a gala affair. She would dress in the latest fashions prevalent in Bombay and bring us the latest Pat Boone 78 rpm records. Occasionally she would bring a friend along and we would gape and gawk at the two glamour queens.

Next came Tosh, the thin, dark and gangly one. She was named Santosh, meaning 'peace' and 'contentment', because after she was born my grandmother, who had been looking forward to the birth of a son, joined or rather smacked her hands in front of Lord Shiva, the household deity, and said, "Hey Bhagwan[7], two girls are more than enough... now let me be at 'peace' and make the next one a boy."

As children, Tosh and I were quite naturally the closest to each other, but to this day she holds a grudge against our mother, who she says always chided and taunted her for having a dark complexion. I don't think it was ever as serious an issue as she made it out to be because Tuti, the youngest, was also a dark child and she aired no such complaint of discrimination ever in her life. However, I admit that a young girl could be more sensitive, and Tosh could never forgive our mother for her 'step-motherly' treatment. The aunt seized this opportunity to ingratiate herself with Tosh who soon became her ardent supporter.

However, what was most surprising was how in her teens, Tosh turned fair as a peach almost overnight! It's a mystery I have never been able to solve. Or it could have been the result of any number of turmeric poultices, or cream skimmed off milk and applied to her face, or *multani mitti*[8] packs, that

---

[7] God.

[8] Fuller's earth.

did the trick. Or maybe God answered her prayers for, by the time she finished school, Tosh looked as fair and fresh as the white daisies that grew wild on the hillside.

After Tosh, came I, who sent off a grand uncle to his choleric death so unceremoniously. I, the son of a mango. A few years following me came Tuti, who was christened Mrinalini. Where they dug out that name from I have no clue. Even after it was shortened to Mrinal, it still got the tongue in a twist. She was born a brat and remained one, using her status as the youngest in the family to get what she wanted. A wild one, she flew the coop as soon as she finished school. As a child, she was dark but had plump, rosy cheeks of the hill children. Later, she had a chequered life, two husbands that I know of, and then went on to live a life of happy singledom somewhere in the countryside of England.

That completes the introduction to the 'Sharmas' of Dil Bahar, commanding a retinue of six servants and, at any given point of time, a pack of three or four dogs. A motley crew who in their individual ways, rocked and ruled Happy Valley.

Chapter 6

Hide-n-Shriek

Surprisingly, not much comes to mind about the days that followed our arrival in Mussoorie. All I can recall is that since it was nearing the end of July, monsoon was in full swing and we couldn't see the sun for many days. For the next eight carefree months we were left to our own devices to do as we pleased. I know we played a lot of hide-n-seek for there were plenty of tricky places to hide in and around the rambling house.

On one such rainy afternoon, we were holed up indoors and got restless. The eldest amongst us chose to bury her nose in a book and refused to play our silly games. So my other two sisters did their usual 'eeny-meeny-mynaa-mo' routine to decide who would hide and who would be the 'den'. The elder of the two, who was the 'den', had to count loudly to 100 – that would give us ample time to choose our hiding place before she could shout "I'm c-o-m-i-n-g!"

My hiding place got easily exposed because my shoes could be spotted from under the curtains, and I was pounced upon with a loud shriek and dragged out. The two of us then began crooning "Tu-uuti, where are youu-uuu, we are coming to get you," as we quickly divided territories and tried to find the youngest one. I bounded up the stairs. My sister scooted off to the grounds.

We turned into every corner of the house. We looked under the beds, we rattled the curtains, and we looked behind trees. No sign of Tuti. No smothered giggles. We asked our mother, our aunt, our servants, if they had seen Tuti. No one had. We got scared. We went pale. It no longer remained a game.

Suddenly, a thought flashed through my mind. There was one place we hadn't looked. There was a small storeroom tucked away under the staircase that we didn't ever bother to explore. Our mother would usually keep the *aatta*[1] there in a huge tin trunk along with cans of rice, other grains and pulses. I ran towards it and opened the door. "I bet you are hiding here, you little witch!" I yelled. Sure enough, giggles sounded from within the trunk of aatta. I unlatched and lifted the lid and there was Tuti, covered in flour. "You stupid idiot!" I screamed, "What made you choose this horrible place? If it hadn't luckily struck me that you might be here, you would have choked to death in that box by now." Tuti, of course, didn't grasp the impact of what I was suggesting and, dusting her frock and giggling uncontrollably, ran off shrieking, "I won! I won!"

All the noise and hysteria had brought our mother running to the scene, and she grabbed Tuti's arm and yelled, "*Chudail, tu saara aatta barbaad kar ditta ai mera!*"[2] Tuti couldn't care a toss and skipped off. From that day onwards, there was always a big, pendulous lock on the door of the storeroom. Chillingly, shrieks rent the house again late one windy night.

Although the house had eight bedrooms, we kids shared our bedroom with our grandmother and aunt. Our elder sister, Raj, who was ten years old at that time, slept in an adjoining bedroom, all by herself. She had this rather peculiar habit of singing to herself with her head buried under the quilt at nights. Above her head was a medium-sized cupboard built into the wall

---

[1] Ground flour.

[2] You little 'Witch', you have ruined all my flour!

in which she kept all her girly things. As the eldest, she thought she was the cat's whiskers and generally kept aloof from us. I remember she always wore her hair in two oily plaits that would be looped and tied with ribbons to hang over her shoulders. Occasionally, she would have her friend Rita, our Goan neighbour's daughter who lived a slope away from our house, come over to spend the night at our place. Rita, or Reeta as we called her, was a tall, dark, knock-kneed girl who would sing English songs that we didn't yet know.

One night, as the clock gonged the witching hour, there came a sudden rattling sound on the windowpanes. My aunt, who was flipping the pages of a Hindi magazine, looked startled and quipped in a scared voice, "What was that?" My grandmother caustically remarked that it was the sound of tree branches brushing against the window pane and told her to put aside her magazine and get to sleep. A few moments later, there it was again, the same sound, albeit louder and more ominous this time. A handful of gravel hit and scattered off the windowpanes. My Bua jumped out of bed, snapped the curtains aside and let out a shrill scream, 'Bhoot, Bhoot!!'[3] I looked out the window and saw two forms with white sheets clumsily draped over them, scrambling down the sloping tin ledge. A few minutes later, I felt the urge to pee and got up to go to the bathroom that was attached to my eldest sister's bedroom. As I tiptoed past her bed, where she and Rita were curled up under the quilts, I could hear them stifling their laughter. Rita, unable to contain it, actually let out a loud snort! I quietly did my business and went back to bed, furious at the way these two morons had scared the shit out of us, but also perversely glad because they had given our aunt the fright of her life and she, who was already anaemic, had turned visibly white as a sheet! But I kept quiet, for if I had complained, my sister would have got her hide whipped,

---

[3] Ghost, Ghost!

while Rita would have been told, in no uncertain terms by my grandmother (who disliked her because she was a non-Hindu and wore her frizzy hair like today's Afro hairdo), never to show her face again in the house.

Our days flitted by like butterflies on wing.

Chapter 7

Three Good Men

The first one was simply called *Paayi*, which means a 'man'. He was a forty-something *sardar*[1] whose beard had turned as white as his turban. The second was Prem, a scrawny fellow who was always looking here and going there – meaning he had a squint in his right eye, made worse by a snowy cataract. And to think he was only twenty-four or thereabouts. The third of the trio was Prem's brother, Babu, who as a boy of twelve had been visited by *Mata*, a reference to Goddess Durga, but also used for those afflicted by the smallpox. Mata was not just a euphemism for the dreaded pox that left untreated could easily kill off people in the early nineteenth century. Yet, absurd as it may sound, it was generally believed that to be visited by the Mata was a sign of divine intervention!

Babu was a survivor. In my mother's words, "He was a sturdy and strong-willed runt of a boy, a real *badmaash*[2]." When it became apparent that 'Mata' had descended on Babu, our grandmother promptly had him cast out of the house and into the *kothri* – a small, dark, abandoned room near the stables where he was to stay during the course of his illness, or perish.

---

[1] A member of the Sikh community.
[2] Rascal.

She couldn't be less bothered. Rather uncharitable behaviour for one who went about barefoot in the belief that it pleased God no end, and was always muttering 'Hari Om, Hari Om'[3] when she was not berating my mother for some imagined slight to herself or her daughter.

But I mustn't digress. Poor Babu lay alone on a straw mat in the dark kothri, his eyes swollen and shut tight by the blisters on his eyelids. My mother says they covered his whole body and she was the only one who would go near him, bathe him, swab his blisters with potassium permanganate mixed with water, and feed him. Now, why couldn't his brother Prem have done that? Simply, because my grandmother forbade him to go anywhere near his brother. In time, the blisters turned into dark brown scabs and as they started to fall off his body, my mother would carefully sweep them up in a piece of cloth and set them afire. This way, the dreaded 'Mata' revealed her 'gentle' side and spared the life of young Babu, but not before leaving her indelible imprint on him in the form of pitted scars. His face always reminded me of the perforated vessels we had in the house, of beaten copper and brass. Babu, when he had fully recovered, wasn't much the worse for his brush with death and neither did he seem to be bothered by his pockmarked face. He was the cheeriest and most insolent of servants we had. His squinty brother on the other hand was a total wimp.

Paayi, whom I spoke of earlier, was a veteran of World War II. He was the village runaway who would sew footballs and polish cricket bats and hockey sticks in my father's sports goods manufacturing unit. Everyone it seemed manufactured sports goods in Sialkot. Paayi, however, at some point between sandpapering and polishing bats had made up his mind to join the army and quietly slipped away without informing anyone. Which army did this unlettered lad join?

---

3 Chanting the name of Hari, which is one of the names of Lord Vishnu.

Of course, the National Army of Subhash Chandra Bose! My grandmother took rather kindly to Paayi, for she would occasionally tell us anecdotes about his Prisoner-of-War status – he had been held prisoner in a German or Japanese camp, I forget which, for a few months. A Congress Party activist, who had once been caught shouting slogans against the British in a 'women's only' procession, my grandmother had once been at the receiving end of their batons – she had even spent a night or two in jail! She wasn't named Durga Dai[4] for nothing! She thus saw a kindred spirit in Paayi and after he returned as a medalled POW to India, followed by a brief visit to the village to meet his wife and kids, he was back to polishing bats and sewing footballs in gunnysacks at my father's yard, to be shipped to Britain.

Paayi had the breeziest smile under his thick white moustache. He laughed heartily at almost anything and everything, in sharp contrast to the permanent frown and screwed-up nose that my grandmother wore on her leathery, timeworn face. Just in case you think I am biased, let me also state that when she was in a particularly good mood, my grandmother would crack a wonderful smile – her walnutty-wrinkled skin would stretch and then what a transformation would come over her face! It could positively glow and beam and I would actually see the sun shine through her otherwise beady, but now twinkling, eyes that would crinkle up with inner joy.

These were the three family retainers who, rather than return to their wives in the villages after the partition of the country, threw in their lot with my father and escaped with us into the forested retreat in Mussoorie. Somehow, each woman in the family seemed to claim one of them as her favourite and trusted confidante. My grandmother smiled on Paayi; my aunt latched on to Prem; and my mother favoured pockmarked

---

[4] A synonym for Devi or Goddess.

Babu. All the while, there were behind-the-scenes intrigues to snatch away Babu, whom my mother had apparently tied to her dupatta. Nothing worked. Finally, it was the lure of a bride that drew Babu away from the hills and dales of Mussoorie to the blistering plains of a remote village near Amritsar. We would never see his face again; not ever.

The next one to go was Paayi, who hadn't even seen the face of his son born five years earlier. Homesickness, filial love, and no doubt a life of freedom in the fields, claimed him. Prem, the squinty-eyed trusty, chose to remain behind, bound no doubt, in some undefined way to my aunt. He must have thought his departure too would amount to an act of desertion of the plain-looking princess, who remained unwed.

New faces arrived to fill in the vacant slots left by the other two. My mother, using her own set of wiles, made sure they would not get entrapped by my grandmother or the aunt. These boys were the fun lot – younger, friskier, and livelier. Three of them were the younger brothers of Bishna, the old chowkidar at the Begum of Rampur's bungalow, whose job was to tend to the fruit trees and the flower beds. As soon as they turned eighteen, they would be sent back to their village because our mother didn't want young, strapping hill lads around her growing daughters. Once the boys got married in the village and spent a year there, they were welcome to return to work at Dil Bahar.

The only lad we weren't allowed to play with was a tall, dark, young boy who was probably at that time in his early twenties. He was Dharmu, the sweeper boy, a pleasant-faced lad whose rather unpleasant duty was to keep the commodes and the toilets clean throughout the day. The flush system for toilets hadn't arrived yet in Mussoorie, and even when it did it never came to Dil Bahar. Life could get real stinky at times! For some odd reason, old Bishna and young Dharmu were the only two servants who wore the white Gandhi cap. Bishna's cap was always crumpled and yellowing, while Dharmu's cap was always spanking white and ironed.

Now when I think of it, Dharmu couldn't have had much of a life serving us, yet serve us he did for a good many years. If he accidentally happened to pass within an inch of my crabbity grandmother, she would immediately cringe, wrap her white cotton dupatta tight around her so that it wouldn't come in contact with him, and make frantic 'get back' gestures with her hand while shouting "*Duur hutt, duur hutt!*"[5] muttering demeaning words at him. In the unfortunate event that the edge of her dupatta brushed him, she would run towards the bathroom mouthing curses at him, to wash both the dupatta and herself from the imagined contamination. Poor Dharmu. I wish I had played with him more often, or at least spoken nicely to him, now and then. And now a long-forgotten snippet comes to my mind: Dharmu belonged to Bijnor, a small town in Uttar Pradesh.

By the time I was fifteen, several hill lads, including Bishna's brother and son, namely Bahadru and Tuyyian, and another young boy called Chandru, the one with two buckteeth, had passed in and out of the gates of Dil Bahar. Then came Satya, Sanjay, and Mohan. All of them were very amiable. However, the boy who guided me one summer afternoon into the delightful art of self-exploration was Bahadru as he showed that my little *nunnu*, to use an Indian euphemism, was made for more than just pissing. Just as one swallow does not make a summer, once was not enough. There followed many more splendoured afternoons on our way back from school. When Bahadru went on a year-long leave to his village, Satya stepped in and took over the delightful role.

A loyal boy, Satya was definitely not a snitch. One evening as we were fooling around, he caught me in a neck clinch from

---

5 Get away, get away!

which there seemed no escape. So, I gave a back-kick that caught him right between his jewels. I was suddenly free and gasping for breath, while he doubled over and howled in pain. His face appeared to be suffused with blood and tears of pain welled into his eyes. I panicked and 'ssshhhhed' him. He was clutching his balls and moaning '*Mein marr raha huon.*'[6] Young as I was, I told him to stop clutching his balls and sat him under a tap and let the cold water run over them till the pain began to subside. Then I promised to let him ride my red racing bike tomorrow if, and only if, he wouldn't go and complain to my parents about the kick I had given him.

---

[6] I am dying.

Chapter 8

Frosted Leaves, Apricot Blossoms

The warm, peaty, sickly-sweet smell that arises with the first showers from the wet earth and rotting leaves can be more intoxicating than most perfumes. Walking around the hills in the rain is like walking in a dream sequence of a Hindi film, where lovers float and embrace in slow motion to some romantic number, through mist generated by a smoke machine off-screen. I have a feeling that the on-screen mist must be hazardous to health in contrast to the mountain mist that can be so refreshing and invigorating. The mountain mist clings to one's hair in fine droplets and settles on woollen sweaters that get soaked fast if they aren't shaken off, right away. At times, the mist rises so thick, one can't see the path beneath one's feet, or the outstretched arm in front of the nose. I would open my mouth wide to suck in the mist and gulp it down deep into my lungs.

When returning from school if I got caught in a heavy shower, I would shut my umbrella while walking through the forest and get properly wet. Passing a drain that ran along the road, just about ready to overflow with the pelting rain, I would jump into it and struggle to take a step forward in the gushing waters. What a thrill that gave, even though I was a lightweight and ran the risk of being swept away by the strong current.

The rains usually ended around end-September and then two things happened. One, the tourists from Bengal began arriving and, two, the leaves started to turn yellow, orange and then gradually a shade of rust, after which the trees would begin to shed them. Autumn, quickly followed by Fall, was no doubt one of the more harmonious seasons in our hill station. This was also the time for the annual Mussoorie Autumn Festival, although sometimes it would skip a year or two. It wasn't particularly festive. There would be the usual painting exhibitions (ghastly, amateurish stuff that any self-respecting wall would shudder to display. Once, even I was persuaded to submit two oils that won a place of pride after my family pulled a few strings, but unfortunately they won no prize). The festival also featured *qawwali*[1] performances with contrived *jugalbandis*[2], skating competitions, *kavi sammelans*[3] etc. We also had dog shows but none of our dogs could be presented, as they failed to match up to the pedigreed species. The best part of the festival were the colourful lights strung along the Mall, and that made our town look lovely at night.

Once the trees had shed most of their leaves, the frost would begin to settle. The limp and ragged leaves would then get frozen stiff with a glaze of frost that sparkled like tiny diamonds and would go crunch-scrunch when we stepped on them. At the first sign of hail, tourists would vanish to wherever they had

---

[1] Qawwali is a form of Sufi devotional music popular in South Asia, particularly in the Punjab and Sindh regions of Pakistan, Hyderabad, Delhi, and other parts of northern India. The poetry is implicitly understood to be spiritual in its meaning, even though the lyrics can sometimes sound wildly secular, or outright hedonistic. The central themes of qawwali are love, devotion and longing (of man for the Divine).

[2] Poetic question-answer retorts or repartee.

[3] Gathering of poets.

come from. This was also the time of our final exams. Over in a week to ten days, they would get rounded off with a big bonfire and marked Christmas celebrations with the singing of carols, nativity plays, and goodbyes of the boarders who would leave the hill town for their homes in the plains. Skating rinks would close; cinema halls would down their shutters; the fancier hotels and restaurants would call it a day. A sure sign that winter was just round the corner.

Coolies, their faces and hands blackened with coal dust and their backs bent over with the weight, would arrive carrying baskets loaded with *patthar ka koyla*[4] and *lakdi ka koyla*[5] to light up winter stoves. *Maunds*[6] and maunds of wood would also arrive for the cooking fires. If that ran short, one could always ask the servants to lop a few branches off the apricot and walnut trees. Sweaters, mufflers, gloves and berets, whose knitting had begun a few months earlier would get pulled out of their trunks. And so would the rubber hot water bottles to keep our beds warm during the early hours of the night for by daybreak, they also turned into freezing bottles. At the first touch of cold rubber, the water bottle would be kicked sleepily from out and under the quilt, on to the dhurried floor.

Call it a quirk of nature, but I remember that the season's first snowfall usually occurred during the night. We would wake up thinking we had overslept into the day; check the time that read eight or eight-thirty and then blink again at the dazzling brightness filtering in through the curtained windows. Drawing them aside, we would see everything blanketed in snow. Pure, driven snow unmarred and unruffled by human footprints. The branches of trees swung real low, unable to bear the burden of four inches of snow piled on them.

---

4 Stone coal.
5 Wooden coal.
6 Units for measuring weights.

I vividly recall that the winter of 1957 was particularly severe. During the course of one night, the snow piled four feet high on the ground. When my mother got up in the morning to go into the kitchen that was located outside the main house, she could not push open the door. She called out to the servants who were still fast asleep in their quarters below the kitchen. Looking back, it really seems silly that we did not have a telephone line running down to the servants' quarters, or even some kind of a bell system to summon them in case of an emergency. So there we were, huddled in our beds without our morning mug of steaming hot tea.

Finally, after yelling herself hoarse and joined by my father who yelled louder than her, we heard a scraping of a spade against the door. The servants were clearing it away so the door could be opened. They had, in a rare moment, used their brains to prepare tea, and now brought that in. Even the dogs were given hot tea to lap up from their bowls. When we went to the bathroom to brush our teeth, there was no water flowing from the taps. The main water pipe that ran along the road above the house had burst and the water gushing from it had frozen into a glorious ice fountain sometime during the night. Its frozen bubbles reflected a myriad rainbow forms in the sunlight. That winter, we formed sleds, which were just plain planks of wood without any ropes to serve as brakes, and carried them right up the steep climb that led from the house to the main road. Once there, we would turn around, sit on the planks and come sliding helter-skelter down the slope using our hands, knees and feet to control the makeshift sled as it sped and slid down the slope raising a flurry of snow in the process.

Meals would be served in the kitchen, as by the time the food was taken to the dining room, it would turn ice cold. But for some odd reason, tea would always be taken in the dining room. Double tea cosies would be pulled over the kettles to keep the tea warm. The *pakodas*[7] would be fried in the ante room and not in the kitchen as they had to be served piping hot. What we really looked forward to, however, was sitting around the stove in the afternoons and devouring melted *gudh*[8] in which almonds, walnuts and cashew-nuts had been dipped. The jaggery-coated nuts made a tasty snack – our mother's speciality. We would all be given newspaper sheets on which she would ladle out portions of this delectable mix. Why it was newspapers and not a porcelain dish, I could never figure out, especially as the hot gudh would stick to the newspaper and we had a frustrating time trying to get the last scraps of the nutty mixture off the paper!

Winters were, and have continued to remain for me, the best season in Mussoorie. Even now whenever I plan a short visit to my hometown, I make sure I visit during December to February. It's bitterly cold, my body really can't take the biting wind any longer, after years spent in Mumbai. Yet I brave it and, wrapped in layer upon layer of clothing, love to spend a few days there in the comfort of my friend's home at Mullingar up in Landour.

Spring would slowly and silently creep up on us around mid-February. When we were watchful, we would notice the tiniest of green leaves trying to push their way along the hillside. The apricot trees would also start sprouting clusters of leaves and buds that would gradually start to open in the days that followed. Bright yellow flowers would burst forth like little bright suns from their cracks and crevices. The sky would turn bluer, and fluffy white clouds would replace the grim grey of winter. Among the first early birds of spring to hop chirruping from branch to branch, would be the Robin with its red breast. Whether it caught any worm or not (that is, if Robins do indeed catch worms!) I don't know.

---

[7] Vegetable fritters served as savory snacks.
[8] Jaggery.

Come March, and the apricot trees would be in full bloom with clusters of delicate, powder-pink flowers. The sole apple tree in the terraced fields alongside our house would get laden with white apple blossoms. Around us, life would begin to renew itself in the most beautiful ways. We would be a year older too as we stepped into our new classes on the first day of school in new shoes, armed with new schoolbags, a new bottle of ink if not a new fountain pen and, of course, new textbooks and crisp, crackling notebooks. There was a spring in our step and a feeling of lightness in everything we did over the coming month. It was as if everything and everyone had been reborn, even though this cycle of seasons repeated itself, year after year. Teachers would smile more, parents would be relaxed and not strict about studies, servants would be more active and not so sluggish... even our dogs would be friskier at this eventful time of the year.

All this would ultimately fall into a routine once summer marched upon spring with the arrival of April. By mid-May, the town would again be bustling with the arrival of the early tourists from Bombay, who would be seen swaggering on the Mall Road dressed in what seemed to us 'Hill Billys', the latest atrocities in fashion. To them, we must have appeared like creatures from a place that time and fashion both forgot to take in their stride.

The Bombay crowd would be overtaken in June by the arrival of the brash Delhi-ites and the two would sometimes clash at the skating rink over a plain 'Jane' from the plains. God forbid if any of the outsiders happened to hit upon a local girl. Out would come our boys armed with hockey sticks, cricket bats and cycle chains. A couple of hotels would organise their individual Miss and Mr. Mussoorie contests, so in a given month we often had three or four Miss Mussoories floating about with their heads held high in the clouds. The fitness bug hadn't yet bitten the youth, so there would be some plump Miss Mussoories and some pot-bellied Mr. Mussoories selected purely on their family's personal rapport with the owner of the hotel concerned. To my knowledge, none of the local girls, or boys, ever entered such a contest. Such forwardness, we were told, only befitted the corrupt youth of the plains.

Although summers got fairly hot under the collar, no home, rich or middling, had a ceiling or a table fan. A refrigerator and an air conditioner were unseen and unheard of. Forty years later, when I returned to Mussoorie for a short break to holiday with my friends, the fan had still not made its advent in their house, although the refrigerator had. What has changed for the worse is that hand-drawn rickshaws have been replaced by cycle rickshaws – the kind you see in Chandni Chowk in Delhi. Cars that get special permits are allowed on the Mall that was earlier completely out of bounds for motorists.

Yet, as they say, the more a town changes, the more it remains the same. And so, there is still enough of Mussoorie of the early 1950s that survives to this day and revives the nostalgia of what this grand old Queen of the Hills was when we were young... once upon a time.

Chapter 9

The Pumpkin and The Beanstalk

A month before the first soft, flannel-grey clouds would float across the pale blue summer skies over Mussoorie, the Cuckoo, otherwise a drab looking bird, would melodiously start her aria of "Cuk-cuk-ooo... cuck-cuk-oo" from her well-screened perch in the tree that grew outside my sister Raj's bedroom. Every day, it would warble and woo the rain that seemed to be in no particular hurry to heed its call to drench it in the cooling shower. Although its courtship of the rain god did at times jangle my nerves, especially when I would be sleeping late into the morning on weekends, I never thought it wise to tell the servants to shoo the bird away. For weren't we waiting as anxiously as the bird was for the first showers that would douse and cool the sweltering earth?

Ever since our lovely hill station had lost much of its once dense forest cover to the reed-thin, giraffe-like Mr. Rawat (who was as unscrupulous as Shylock, reminding us of that character from Shakespeare's *Merchant of Venice*) and his lumbering woodcutters, the summers had grown longer and the monsoon shorter.

No one quite knew the antecedents of Mr. Rawat except that he would hibernate at Saharanpur in the winters and show up as soon as the snows had melted around the end of March. For all his ungainly height, skeletal frame, thin and long giraffe-like neck with its protruding Adam's apple, and that awful toothbrush moustache, he looked very dapper in formal trousers and a sleeveless woollen sweater as he loped around the hillside with an enigmatic smile that always hovered around the corners of his mouth. It was as if he was getting an endless orgasm as he strode around chewing on the *paans*[1] that he carried in his pockets. He knew that the residents hated the very sight of him, and the children sniggered behind his back and chanted '*Giraffe aaya, Giraffe aaya,*'[2] whenever we spotted him. But he never broke his long stride and seemed impervious to our disdainful glares and rude remarks. He was decidedly a loner. I don't remember ever seeing him in the company of another person from the town.

Why did everyone dislike him, especially the children? I haven't been able to fathom that. In fact, I haven't given him a thought all these years. So why would I be telling you about him now? Is it because a person who appears so 'different' from us, behaves unlike us, and does not conform to acceptable norms of appearance and social intercourse, unwittingly leaves an impression on your mind? Anyway, Mr. Rawat went about his business of denuding the hills without anyone realising what damage he was inflicting or even raising murmurs of disapproval at his single status at the age of thirty-two, plus or minus a few years.

One summer, word went around that Mr. Rawat was stricken with typhoid and the gossip mills wasted no time in gleefully sharing this bit of the man's misfortune with everyone who cared to listen. A month passed, then two, and yet there was no sight

---

[1] Betel nut leaves covered with a dash of limepaste and kattha, an extract from the bark of the Acacia tree, stuffed with cardamom, shredded betelnut and coconut, etc. and folded into small triangles.

[2] Giraffe has come, Giraffe has come.

of the man. Finally, the news floated up from the plains that he was recovering and recuperating in the warmer climes of his hometown. He was spotted one day in town, after the monsoon had bid us a hasty goodbye, looking like a scarecrow. How could anyone as thin as Mr. Rawat get any thinner? Well, he did. It was as if a gypsy woman had put the thinning curse on him in the manner of another gypsy woman in Stephen King's *Thinner*.

Strangely enough, it was at this point of his near-invisibility that Margaret Larkins, our piano teacher who was fat as one could possibly be (yet like most fat people, also amazingly light and swift on her feet), spied on Mr. Rawat one evening as he opted for a shortcut that took him past her cottage. For her it was love at first sight, or so we thought. I'm sure the gossip mills may well have a different story to tell. Maggie, as she was called, was then a spinster living with her parents, and she had recently celebrated her thirty-fifth birthday. I recalled that bit because just a few weeks ago we had all sung an off-key 'Happy Birthday' to her during our piano lesson. In contrast to Mr. Rawat, Maggie was a jolly old lass whose face was always wreathed in bouncy, brown curls; lips painted a vivid scarlet; a peaches-and-cream complexion that was without a blemish and offset by large loops of brilliantly coloured earrings. Her short, podgy fingers would nimbly and effortlessly roll out Beethoven or Chopin symphonies when she balanced her ample, broader-than-a-beam backside on the tiny, rotating piano stool and would sway left and right, forward and backward as the music flowed through her fingers.

Maggie lived with her aged parents in a bungalow just below the school. As one of her favourite protégés who also, at that age, happened to sing loud and clear in a rising soprano, I would often drop in at her cottage on my way home to say 'hi-hullo' to her dad. Old man Larkins always had a pipe in his hand or mouth, and wore a beret to keep his head warm or to hide his balding pate. Maggie would bring out a teacake her mother

47

had baked and a drink of orange squash, which was the most popular beverage of the day. Although he had a rather gruff way of speaking, Maggie's dad was quite a gentle-hearted man. Once, Maggie had told him that I was an avid stamp collector and he asked to see my collection. When I told him they were all loose and jumbled up in a box, he rolled his eyes towards the ceiling and looked as if he would have a mild stroke!

He said, "Ask your father to buy you a stamp album and some packets of hinges and bring them to me. I will paste them nicely for you in the stamp album and then you can keep adding to them."

Now that I think of it, Maggie actually did a lot to help me grow out of my shell. She made me join the Pen Pal club she formed and christened as The Shamrock Club. We made badges cut out of cardboard in the shape of a shamrock leaf, painted them green and pinned them to our shirt front whenever a meeting was scheduled of the Shamrockers. Besides teaching me the piano and preparing me for the exams held by the Trinity College of Music, Dublin, she would give me solo lines to sing – I being the only boy in the choir who was not shy in the company of girls from junior and senior school.

She shepherded me into the Nativity plays we used to enact just before the school shut down in mid-November and, once, even induced me into giving a solo *Kathak*[3] recital on the school's Annual Day!

One funny incident stands out among all these other activities. I was five years old when, one afternoon, six of us, five girls including my older sister, and myself, were sitting cross-legged on the wooden floor around Maggie, who was seated at the piano, and putting us through the music scales in preparation for an upcoming concert. While the girl sitting to the right of

---

[3] A classical Indian dance form of North India.

me, a princess from one of the royal estates, was busy picking her nose, I, quite unconscious of the fact, had my hand inserted into my shorts and was twiddling with my pee-pee. Maggie happened to swing around on her stool just then and she pulled on a frown and said, "*Baba*⁴, take your hand out from there... right now!" I didn't quite get what she was saying and kept twiddling. She repeated, more sternly this time, "Baba, I am talking to *you!*" Then exasperated, she turned to my sister and told her, "Santosh... tell him, in your language, to take his hand out from there!" and all the girls began to snigger and titter!

One day, we heard that Maggie was marrying the reed-thin Mr. Rawat. She disappeared for a fortnight from the school after telling us that we had to practise our piano lessons every afternoon, regardless. That was the last time I saw her in a cleavage-revealing white blouse and her tight black skirt. When she returned to work, she was a transformed woman, wearing a bright red and gold sari, a matching *choli*, *mangalsutra* and *bindi*.⁵ Maggie, in her new avatar, had been rechristened Madhuri! This time, it was our turn to get a mild stroke! All the same, they looked every inch Mussoorie's odd couple as they stepped out holding hands and gliding along the Mall.

Gone were the teacakes and the orange squash as Mr. Thin moved bag and baggage into Maggie's house, soon after their wedding. I wondered if his legs would dangle from the knees down over the footboard of the bed – he was *that* tall. My imagination then went into overdrive. What if she rolled over him one night and smothered him to death under her weight? Anyway, no matter how hard she must have tried to get Mr. Rawat to put on some flesh on his bony frame, he never gained an ounce. (The measure of weight was all in pounds and ounces since the metric system had not yet been introduced.)

---

4 Baba, in this case, refers to a young boy.
5 Blouse, black bead necklace worn by married woman; red dot on forehead, also a sign of marital status for a Hindu woman.

Sometime later, after I had changed schools, Maggie and Mr. Rawat dropped by at our home one evening to bid us goodbye. Maggie had resigned from her post as music teacher and was moving down to the plains of Saharanpur. My mother presented her with one of her unworn saris and a token gift for her husband, while my father asked her to give one last recital on the piano in our living room. Sweet Maggie looked at her husband who nodded his assent, and played a beautiful piece of music.

Two summers later, we heard Madhuri was back as Maggie. She had left Mr. Rawat, or vice versa. Gone were the sari and bindi. Back came on the frilly white blouses and the tight black skirts. I'm not sure whether I was glad for her, but I definitely wasn't sad. That man did her no good and did not deserve her. When I returned to Mussoorie after a decade or so, I happened to catch sight of him loping down the Mall, wearing a checked, tweed jacket, loose pants that flapped around his ankles, and puffing on a pipe. His raven black hair had now greyed at the temples and he stooped as he walked.

I do remember Maggie's father died because I vaguely recall attending his funeral. Soon after that, she vacated her cottage and, along with her mother, moved back to Saharanpur where she took up a job as a music teacher in a school. Whenever I cross Saharanpur on my way to Mussoorie, I think of her – maybe she is sitting on a rotating piano stool and playing the 'Devil's March' for which she was once rebuked sternly by the Mother Superior of our school.

Chapter 10

The Tiger under My Bed

Eyes as round as saucers stuck out of a face that looked as if he had run smack into a wall or had it pushed-in by a forceful palm. Long, silken, tawny hair covered his body. Barely eight inches high and eighteen inches long, he waddled slowly on his paws. This was the peke my father brought home one day from I don't know where. Our first ever pet, he was fussed over by everyone, but most of all by my father who taught him to relish fried pakodas, tandoori chicken and a whole lot of other goodies dogs are not supposed to have. The peke was none the worse for them; he thrived and fell in love with my father. Of all the things he would relish, he loved my mother's hot *chappati churi* that consisted of two hot, hand-crushed chappatis kneaded with ghee and sprinkled with sugar. That was his usual lunchtime treat.

In my twelfth year, I developed thirty-one-day typhoid fever. Tiger, as we had named him, just slunk under my bed and did not budge from there until I completely recovered. My mother would serve his meal on a plate slid under the bed, and he ate it there. I think the only time he slipped out was when he wanted to piss or shit. Contrary to his name, he never growled, barked or snapped at strangers. He was a quiet, sober dog who, a few years later, just lay down and died in his sleep one cold, wintry night.

He was lifted and buried in a quiet little muddy pathway that ran down some way below the grounds of the house.

The mid-50s saw a rash of *I Love Lucy* movies starring the irrepressible Lucille Ball who became one of the most loved comediennes of the silver screen. Lucille, hard to pronounce by Indians, was quickly shortened to Lucy that rolled easily off the tongue. It became the new craze – while a lot of Christian girls were named Lucy, some Indian girls were also given the same *nom de plume*. It even became the name of choice for female cats and dogs!

A few days after Tiger died, a full-grown female German shepherd came into our home. She was promptly named Lucy by us. I do vividly remember that she came with our old sweeper. He told us to keep her tied down for a couple of days so she would get used to her new environment, otherwise she would run away in search of her old master, who had died a few days ago of old age.

Dogs love children, and Lucy was no exception. Over the next few days she warmed up to the four of us and helped us get over the loss of Tiger. This slim and rather elegant lady was soon mated with a pedigreed German Shepherd and delivered a litter of five woolly pups, one of whom was black as the devil! This was also the first time I was exposed to the miracle of birth-giving. When I peeped into the room where she slept – Lucy was half-way into delivering her fifth pup. One of those died. Two were given away to friends. Two remained with us – *Kaalu*, the black devil, and *Bhuru*, the brownie. Kaalu grew up to be a stay-at-home type while Bhuru turned out to be a vagabond who was always loitering around and sometimes did not return home for the night. He would usually get an earful and a few whacks with the stick from my mother. His escapades proved fatal one night when a leopard tracked him and carried him off to his jungle lair.

One thing I hadn't been able to figure out all these years was why our parents chose to give their dogs away after loving and feeding them for a couple of years. But now, suddenly, an answer comes to mind from out of the blue. I think that after Tiger's death, they couldn't bear the thought of another dog dying on them.

Another thing I have just realised is that my father must have been quite a dog lover, although after Tiger I really can't recollect him petting any dog, nor was any other dog allowed to sleep under his bed. Strange, isn't it? Still, he liked to have dogs around the house and it wasn't only for the pleasure of his kids. I'm also surprised that my grandmother, who was not enamoured of dogs, never expressed her displeasure as she did for his other quirks and indulgences.

Anyway, one fine morning while reading *The Times of India*, my father's eyes fell on an advertisement under the 'Kennels' section that featured a fluffy white pup in a wicker basket. He reached out for the phone and asked the operator to connect him to the number given in the ad. Those were the days of manually operated telephone exchanges, so the operator of Bikaner exchange in Rajasthan told him she would call back in an hour, when the call connected. The wait did not deter my father.

It was the end of November. Schools had shut down for winter vacations that lasted for over three months, much to our joy and relief. We were sitting around a log fire lit in the cast iron stove in his office, when he told us to fetch Prem, the squint-eyed servant. When Prem entered the room, rubbing his hands together, his squint eye turned toward me but his voice addressed my father.

Prem was asked to travel to Dehradun the next morning to fetch a new-born pup that had been ordered from His Highness of Bikaner. I begged that I also wanted to go, while my sister Tosh, piped in to say she would also like to accompany us. Tuti, the youngest of the lot, who was lying on the sofa as she wasn't quite well, also found her voice to squeal, "*Papaji, minnu vi jaana ai,*" meaning she too should be counted in.

At this point, neither Tosh nor I wanted her to accompany us and ruin our trip. But there was no reasoning with Tuti. She wailed and howled and managed to push her temperature up to 101 degrees. Tosh and I were delighted; my mother got anxious and took Tuti into her bed that night. She was still insisting she wanted to accompany us to Dehradun, so finally we promised her Kwality's Toffees from the plains. She relented and agreed to stay at home.

That night, neither Tosh nor I slept much. We were up a good two hours before the bus was scheduled to leave from Kincraig, the main terminal for buses plying the zigzag road between Mussoorie and Dehradun. On reaching Dehradun, we really didn't quite know how to kill our time, as our appointment with the royal pup was set at four in the afternoon. So, we headed straight for Kwality's restaurant and ordered a hearty breakfast of French fries, potato cutlets, toast smeared with Polson's butter and steaming cups of tea, while we let Prem off to buy tickets for an English movie, *The Wizard of Oz* playing at the Odeon, nearby. When it got over, we met Prem outside the cinema hall and hopped onto a tonga that took us to the White House – a leading hotel in Dehradun. Since our father knew the owner of the hotel, he greeted us with tea and cakes after which we were guided to the room where the pup was resting.

A tall, moustached man wearing the livery of the royal retinue, of what was then the princely state of Bikaner, greeted us with a stiff bow and a *namaste*[1] and bid us to enter. There, near a logwood fire crackling in the fireplace rested a wicker basket on which a white, furry pup, a pure bred pomeranian, slept on a purple velvet cushion. A small red blanket protected him from the winter cold. The tall man put a finger to his lips and whispered "Sshhhhh" indicating that we should not wake up the pup. A baby's milk-feeding bottle lay near the basket.

---

[1] The formal Indian form of greeting.

He handed us an instruction sheet bearing the royal emblem and told us that we must follow the Dos and Don'ts listed down for feeding the pup. Lastly, he pulled out two mini bottles of foreign brandy. "Just half a teaspoonful," he whispered, in case the pup shivered. Prem made the exchange and soon we were in a taxi headed back for Mussoorie.

We took the taxi right up to our house, which was not the done thing, as one usually walked up from Kincraig, but this was a royal pup and had to be handled with care. Besides, it was freezing cold outside. At home, a fire blazed in the room where the rest of the family was seated, awaiting our arrival. My father was highly impressed by the bottle of imported brandy which had been sent along with the pup and immediately proceeded to spoon some into the pup's mouth, but not before he tasted it himself. Tuti demanded her bribe of Kwality's Toffees which we handed to her before she could bawl again. That night, the pup got christened Roy – because I was an avid fan of Roy Roger's cowboy comics and had also caught a few of his movies.

The point to be noted about this episode is that our house was never without dogs. Neither was it without pigeons. From one pair of pigeons my father brought with him one day from Dehradun, their number grew to fifty, as they *gutturr-gooed* – those pigeony sounds they make – and strutted about with thin chests thrust out. A huge twenty-foot by ten-foot wire cage was built in which a dozen-odd boxes with compartments were stacked for these feathered creatures. They would be let out every morning to fly free in the sky and would wing home around sunset following their in-built radar system. Pigeons look horribly ugly when they have just hatched from the eggs but they grow up into beautiful birds. When they are not flapping and flitting around, they are constantly pecking the ground even when there is nothing visible to eat. It's a wonder they don't wear out their beaks! If only human teeth were just as hardy!

Keeping them company was another circular cage that stood on a spindle of wood. Its roof was carved in the shape of a green pagoda and inside the cage were four mini bird-swings. Bright and pastel-hued budgerigars, or love birds as they are called, they chirruped and swung merrily on swings, as if they had been trained at a circus ring. There were also half a dozen hens that provided us with eggs for breakfast and two goats for milk because the doctor had prescribed goat's milk for me. What fun Tuti and I used to have grabbing their teats and squirting their warm milk all over our faces.

As is normal with boys of my age, I also had my own private collection of beetles and lizards, held captive in wooden boxes. The rhinoceros and stag beetles were used to lock horns and stage fights, while the servants and I waged a few annas on the side which appeared likely to win. When I was studying Biology in Grade VI, my teacher, one Mr. Hooper, once handed out butterfly nets to the students. I used mine to collect specimens of colourful Himalayan moths and butterflies. That's how Tuti, Tuyyian – the thirteen-year-old servant boy, and I would be off chasing butterflies on weekends. In the end, I had the most amazing collection, pinned and categorised in a glass-topped wooden box. The most prized was a pale-green moon moth with a wide crescent-shaped wing span.

How could I forget to tell you about Goldie and Orangie? These were the two goldfish that swam and circled the fluted crystal glass bowl for years in our living room. We could never determine which one was male and which female. When they offloaded thin strings of fish-shit, we thought one or the other was laying eggs and kept waiting for baby goldfish to appear – which of course, never did. Who knows, maybe both were male... or both female. After they died, we used the crystal bowl as a lamp that hung from the ceiling and had a blue light bulb that cast a wondrous moonglow at night.

Chapter 11

She Walked in Beauty

She lived in a castle, but not in England or Spain. It was in our very own Mussoorie. The castle, complete with ramparts and turrets, sat atop a rather barren, brown hill and had its own private temple that shone like a pearl. The temple was linked to the castle by a narrow mud and gravel pathway. Whoever conceptualised, designed and built the two monuments must have been inspired by Lord Krishna, as the god was the residing deity, along with his consort Radha, of that temple.

However, what this castle did not have was a moat and a drawbridge and I often wondered why the architect had chosen to do away with these essentials. In the early days, when the road to the castle was spread with gravel, the commoners were allowed to climb the steep pathway once a year and that was on *Janamashtami*, the stormy night of Lord Krishna's birth. On this auspicious day, the private road got thrown open to the public. At one place, it bypassed the castle and narrowed down on its approach to the temple. Sometime in the late 1960s, a macadam path got laid, where the Raja and Rani could drive up in their chauffeur-driven limousine, instead of being pulled up in the royal-crested, two-wheeled rickshaw by five liveried men.

One thing that never ceased to amuse me was the custom-built rickshaws of the royals who had their summer residences in Mussoorie. They came in such funny shapes. One of those, I recall, was built like a baby's pram and had a windshield-like front that treated the occupants of the rickshaw, or should I say royal carriage, to the jogging backsides of the two liveried rickshaw pullers at the front. Another regal rickshaw was shaped along the lines of Cinderella's golden pumpkin. And yet another looked like a palanquin. Royal or no royal, they all had to descend from their carriages at some point on the Mall, where no privately-owned rickshaws were allowed to ply.

Let's return to the castle that stood overlooking Happy Valley. As children, we would get invited to the birthday parties of the prince and princess and got to see what the inside of the castle looked like. In the reception area, drawing room, and dining room, stood or sat stuffed tigers, leopards and bears looking fierce and frightening on their heavy wooden pedestals. On the walls were mounted other hunting trophies, the antlers of stags shot by generations of Rajas. In the photographs that hung on the walls, the royal hunter would invariably be wearing jodhpurs and knee-length boots, holding a gun whose butt would be resting on the animal's head while his other hand would be twirling his moustache. In a couple of glass-fronted racks along the walls, guns and rifles rested horizontally or vertically on velvet rests. French tapestries hung gauzily from vaulted ceilings giving a softly-muted ambience of the palace to princes and princesses not accustomed to facing the stark, harsh realities outside their windows.

In case of this particular royal family, both the prince and princess were rotund butterballs, soft and plump. Overfed and over-pampered, the princess's bedroom appeared to have been pulled straight out of a fairy tale book. Her bed was carved out in the shape of an oval-shaped, pink lotus that appeared to have bloomed right in the centre of the room. A smaller, down-turned lotus rose on a sturdy green stem to provide a protective canopy over the dimpled princess while she slept dreaming probably of jam tarts, mince pies and cookies.

Overhead, the ceiling was hand-painted to recreate the deep blue night sky with a silver crescent moon and stars that glowed in the lamp light. How we envied her that bed! Even her dressing table and stool were in the form of lotuses. Any wonder, she was called Padmavati[1] alias Pinky? Her older brother, on the other hand, just an ounce less plump than her, went by the name of Pratap. While the dimpled Pinky was somewhat of a chatterbox, her brother was the silent and sober sort who would often break into tears when reprimanded by the class teacher. Both studied at our school. 'Prats' as we addressed him, came riding a horse to school, while Pinky trudged along on foot. Such are the ways of Indian parents, who dote on sons and subjugate their daughters to such ignominies. Not that Pinky ever noticed or seemed to mind the exalted status bestowed on her dumb brother.

The womenfolk of the royal family, after entering their teens, were expected to wear chiffon saris. I have yet to see a more elegant fabric than the French chiffon which flows like water upon the feminine form. Their heads were never allowed to go uncovered, at least not in public, and were draped seductively with the pallu of the translucent drape.

The Rani of the erstwhile princely state of Indrapur 'walked in beauty' – to use Lord Byron's phrase. Draped in clouds of misty white, grey, pink and blue chiffons, a tiny diamond nose ring flashed and glittered on her high cheek-boned, oval face, every time it caught the rays of the sun during the day, and the glow of chandeliers at night. Slim yet curvaceous, she was truly the embodiment of grace and beauty. Her raven-black tresses fell to her shoulders in soft waves. In her soft-spoken manner, she would welcome us as we arrived at the prince or the princess's birthday party, and heap presents on us when we left for home.

---

[1] Padma means a lotus.

She would let us sit on the stuffed tigers, leopards and bears, if the Raja was busy elsewhere to notice. In a small garden reserved for afternoon tea parties, a large swing hung on sturdy iron chains from the heavy limb of a mighty *Deodar*[2] tree.

Trailing the Rani was an efficient, suited and booted secretary whose frame was always bent, ever so slightly in a deferential bow. He was a young, handsome man around twenty-seven years of age, far younger of course, than the Raja himself, whom I would put to be around forty-five years old. I had observed that the Rani appeared more serene and relaxed when her secretary was flitting around her. She would even venture a tinkling laugh at something he would murmur in her ear. Rani sahiba I think had a sixth sense that warned her whenever Raja would approach; her back would stiffen and she would immediately put some distance between the secretary and herself.

Several birthdays went by of the prince and princess, along with those of Lord Krishna whose Janamashtami was celebrated with far more pomp and regal splendour as befitted the blue God. His white marble temple would be illuminated with colourful electric bulbs while the dome of his temple would blaze in golden glory under the floodlit lamps. This brilliant jewel was visible from our bungalow that faced the castle from about a kilometre away. After our Janamashtami celebrations at home, we would leave for the temple, accompanied by our aunt and a couple of servants who would be carrying stainless steel platters heaped with marigold garlands, new clothes, and sweetmeats for baby Krishna. The womenfolk gathered there would dance to devotional bhajans extolling the love of Radha and Krishna who stood as mute witnesses to the spectacle that was unfolding before their fixed gaze. At times, I wondered if I had detected an eye or hand movement in the statue of Krishna, but it was probably more wishful thinking than any actual flicker of life

---

2 A species of cedar native to the western Himalayas.

in the blue God. The *prasad*[3] distributed by the panditji of the temple consisted of the usual *laddus*, *pedas*[4] and bananas which always tasted sweeter on Janamashtami than on a regular day. Surprisingly, the dimples in Pinky's cheeks grew deeper over the years and her crooked teeth miraculously straightened under dental care. Whenever his father went out on an early morning ride, Pratap would accompany his sister on foot and and passing by our house, would call out to us. We would run up the slope and together we would all head for school. A time came when I had to change schools and so did Prats. He went off to a school in the plains, while I moved to a co-ed school about six kilometres away from our house.

Out of habit, the royal family would leave the castle when the schools shut down for winter vacations in mid-November. The castle would be shut but we would occasionally go to visit the temple. There, we would visit the Raja's private garden that had a large round pond in which lotuses bloomed and colourful fish swam lazily. This was the time to go and steal some fish from the Raja's pond for our own glass aquarium at home. Ahhh... the pleasures of petty thieving!

Nothing else I think can match the thrill of stealing things as a child. Whether it was books from the local bookshop, furtively hidden in the deep pockets of our overcoats, or sweets from glass jars at sweetmeat stores. While one of us would divert the shopkeeper's attention, another would quickly snatch whatever he/she could lay hands on. Don't get me wrong. The childish prank provided instant relief from the boredom of being shut at home during the long winter days.

In the spring of 1964, Pinky and Prats didn't turn up at school. A month went by, then two, and still they didn't

---

3 Food offerings made to the Gods, later distributed amongst the devotees.
4 Indian sweetmeats.

show up. Neither did Raja and Rani return to their castle on the hill. Curious, our father summoned the temple's panditji on the pretext of holding a puja at home. During the course of that visit, out tumbled skeletons from the royal cupboard. The Raja, it turned out, had chosen to take *sanyas*[5] and decided to abdicate his position to his elder son. This came as quite a shock to us. Who would have thought that a Raja accustomed to wine, women and song would choose this path?

A year or two later, a second skeleton tumbled out of the closet. Apparently, the Rani sahiba after being deserted by her husband, had chosen to elope with the dashing secretary. Neither were ever spotted again in our hometown. To my young mind, their love affair paralleled that of Radha-Krishna.

For many years, thereafter, the castle lay barren.

Its windows were covered with heavy drapes and shut to the outside world.

The swing in the garden stood still on its oaken plank and weeds sprouted high in the flowerbeds.

The water in the fishpond grew murkier and murkier.

As time went by, we couldn't spot any goldfish in it. Probably, unable even to swim in the thick growth of algae and slimy muck, they too had died.

---

[5] Renunciation of worldly pleasures for spiritual pursuits.

Chapter 12

Choirboy, Pianist, Actor...
and an Out-of-Town Dancer

We were three boys in a school full of girls. Dheeraj, Amarjit and I kept each other company from Kindergarten right through Standard Four at the Convent of Jesus and Mary in Mussoorie. All of us were 'Mama's boys' whose mothers wanted their elder daughters to look after their sons in primary school. Dheeraj and I were the brainy ones who never gave the girls in our class a chance to outshine us in any subject. We competed with each other to secure the first or the second rank at the annual exams. Amarjit in contrast would trail far behind the girls and usually come, as the teacher put it, 'first from the last'.

Pampered and cosseted at home, Dheeraj had no talent for anything besides studies, and Amarjit had no talent even for that. I was the one with a dulcet voice and would get chosen to sing in the choir with the girls. Since boys at that age, the ones who can sing that is, can take on the higher contralto notes which even girls can't, Maggie, our music teacher, would single me out to sing a few lines solo in the repertoire. Her favourite was a particular number called 'The Fisherman's Song'. We were instructed to sway left and right to simulate the movement of waves while we sang.

I was the only boy among the three to take up piano lessons from Maggie, I've never quite understood this piano business. Although I was very good at 'reading' music and also good at playing it – my nimble fingers would race over the keys even as I would criss-cross one hand over the other to have them run from one end of the keyboard to the other – Maggie would declare that I had no 'ear' for music. This meant that she would, in preparation for the Trinity College of Music exams, stand me in the corner with my back to her and then strike a chord with one of her plump fingers and ask me to 'name' the note she had just struck! Nine times out of ten, I would give the wrong answer. Exasperated, she would throw up her plump hands in the air and almost fall off the tiny rotating stool she was perched on. If I could read music well, play it well, then why couldn't I identify the note when she struck it? Well, even the examiner had no answer to that!

At the school assembly one fine morning, they announced that the Bishop would be visiting our school to inaugurate the new sports ground. To welcome him, the Reverend Mother asked Maggie to get her act together for a memorable concert. After much mulling, our music teacher selected a sprightly piece of music for me to practise rigorously, until I could play it blindfolded. The nuns were delirious with excitement, rushing around in their swirling black habits, their rosaries clicking and clacking, as they bowed and swept their way instructing which class was to be seated where in the hall on that day.

At last, the eventful day dawned bright and clear. After the lunch break, my sister helped me change out of my school uniform into a white, full-sleeved shirt and long pants, slicked my hair wet with some water and neatly parted it with her girly comb. The Reverend Mother swished in to bless me prior to the performance, and I was hustled by Maggie to the piano kept in the Assembly Hall. She and I had a prearranged signal that would signify the entry of the Bishop in the doorway of the hall, at which particular moment I was to poise both my hands six inches above the keyboard, and bring them crashing down on the keys to strike the opening notes of the music.

Right on cue, Maggie bent her neck to one side and sent me a heavily-mascara-ed wink. That was my signal to strike... and strike I did. From that moment, I barely glanced at the sheets of music, except to indicate to Jill (who had been stationed by the side of the piano to quickly flip the pages), and more or less played the entire piece from memory. Out of the corner of my eye, I could see Maggie from the wings, pointing one fat finger towards my feet but paid no heed. Jill noticed this and discreetly kicked my right foot that apparently was doing a crazy, rhythmic tapping on the wooden floor. After the performance, I was to stand up, get away from the stool and bow to the Bishop who was seated on the stage along with the Reverend Mother and senior nuns. Bow I did, but in doing so cracked the head of Jill, who had also been instructed to do the same. She let out an 'Ouchh!' and I clapped a hand to my head, while the Bishop and the nuns tittered but gave us a round of applause.

Several days later, Maggie came home and told my dad that she thought it would be a good idea for him to buy a piano so I could practise at home, after school. The very next day, a gleaming black piano stood in the living room. It became a showpiece to display to visitors to our house. However, after the initial excitement of having such a grand acquisition that even Dheeraj and Amarjit couldn't boast of possessing, I forgot it was there and left it unused after I changed schools. One day, when we were changing houses, that grand German piano was sold off for a mere five hundred rupees.

Yet, I can boastfully say that I was artistically inclined from the word go. At a very early age, I was painting nudes (an activity quite unheard of or even allowed in a fairly orthodox household in the 1950s). A particular one I remember was copied from

Playboy and featured a voluptuous slave girl posing seductively in chains of gold and a metal bra that revealed more than what it was meant to conceal. Around the same time, my father got it into his head to hire a dance-cum-music teacher to make me a *tabla*[1] maestro and a Kathak dancer.

After school, this old man would visit us three times a week with his young daughter who acted as his assistant. The Kathak part of the exercise resulted, a year later, as a last-minute addition to the annual school concert held for the parents. Knowing that I was learning Kathak, Maggie cajoled me into giving a solo performance with my dance teacher rendering the tabla and his daughter playing the harmonium. To prepare for the performance of a lifetime, my mother went and bought a red brocade sari, a sequin-and-brocade cardboard crown, and a brand new set of *ghungroos*[2]. She also loaned her gold jewellery, which my sister was strictly instructed to handle with care and bring it back after the concert. So, there I was in the piano room getting dressed. Our Hindi teacher came forward to tie the red silk dhoti around my waist. Maggie herself lined my eyes with mascara and applied the lipstick while my sister piled the gold jewellery on me and told me not to move too vigorously onstage lest I drop a precious trinket.

"And now..." announced the girl in charge of emceeing the show, "We bring you a grand Kathak performance by Miss (and here she shamelessly put her hand to her mouth and sniggered stagily) Tara from..." and the rest was drowned out by the claps and whistles from the crowd. The opening notes of the harmonium heaved rustily from the bellows and the tabla drummed out the *taal*, the rhythmic beats of Kathak. The curtains parted down the centre and there I stood frozen in a striking Kathak pose wearing my crown. The dance teacher nodded his head for me to

---

[1] An Indian percussion instrument.

[2] Pads with rows of tiny bells worn on the feet by dancers.

begin, and I stamped my feet in the opening steps of the dance to the rhythm of the tabla. Somewhere towards the end of the performance, I was to execute a series of swirls and twirls without feeling giddy. I swirled and twirled from one end of the stage to the other and sent one part of the pair of ghungroos flying and landing on the tabla. I froze mid-dance, the curtain came down and the audience clapped, thinking it was the end of the performance. Someone whistled and shouted, "*Arrey, iss dancer ko khaas Bombay se bulaya gaya hai!*"[3] Backstage, I was in tears. Maggie rushed towards me and did "Sssshhhhh...," and hustled me off the stage. I was barely twelve and in tears at my ruined performance. But my parents assured me later that everyone had loved my act.

Those were some of the happiest days of my life. Standards One to Four were a riot of fun and laughter. Right through Standard Three, we were only allowed to use pencils and erasers in class. We longed for the days when we would graduate to Standard Four and be allowed to write with fountain pens and ink. Time flew by and before I knew it, it was the evening of my first day in Standard Four. I went out to the market with my father to buy a fountain pen and a bottle of Parker Blue Ink. It was a Doric pen, the most popular brand at that time – which also sponsored weekly prizes on *Binaca Geet Mala*, a top ten Hindi film song programme that was broadcast on Radio Ceylon. (Why it was called Radio Ceylon, I haven't figured out to this day!)

Going to the notice board to check which classroom had been allotted to Standard Four this year, I was absolutely thrilled to note it was the stand-alone classroom that faced the main sports ground – the one that had a merry-go-round and a see-saw. I quickly dashed down the slope towards the playground and ran into the class to occupy the corner desk in the front row.

---

3 This dancer has been specially called from Bombay.

I put my books in the desk, my schoolbag below, and laid my brand new pen in the groove made for pencils and pens on top of the desk. And, I filled some ink into the ink pot that was embedded in the right-hand corner of the desk. Then I went outside and sat on the steps of the classroom to warm myself in the winter sun. Soon, giggling and shrieking "Hi Shiv! Hi Shiv!" the boarder girls started trickling into the classroom.

Jill came and hugged me and I hugged her back. Tara bounced in with her fringe framed on either side by candle-straight brown hair and a smile that pulled the corners of her mouth in a downward curve. Dheeraj came in panting, lugging a heavy schoolbag and mopping his sweaty brow with a crumpled handkerchief. Pramila of the bulging eyes who at ten years of age looked as if she had a case of the thyroid, also came sporting a fringe. It looked as if fringes were the style of the day. Padmini, who looked least like the princess she was, smiled broadly, showing off her missing front tooth.

Then, in walked Miss Bartlett, the teacher we had been hoping and praying would take our class, this year. She came wearing her staple tweed skirt and jacket and kept pushing her spectacles with her middle finger up the non-existent bridge of her nose. She also had a habit of furrowing her forehead in a frown and, simultaneously, widening and then contracting her mouth as if she was always doing some kind of facial exercise. It was an honour to be called out by her to clean the blackboard with a duster and she invariably bestowed it on her favourites in the class.

Besides teaching us the prescribed curriculum, she would also take us out for nature walks and point out the names of the trees, shrubs, and birds, along the route. One afternoon, she rushed into the class clapping her hands and saying, "Come out, come out class... I have something exciting to show you." We all trooped out to see Miss Bartlett pointing her finger up towards one of the Deodar trees outside. "Look there," she squeaked, "Do you see the *Mynah*[4] bird feeding her babies in the nest? There, there... the daddy bird also comes!" she cried, quite beside herself with excitement. That's the first I heard that birds also had Mummys and Daddys. An Anglo-Indian, our teacher could never pronounce Indian words correctly and would occasionally set the Hindus among us into splits of laughter when she pronounced the *Ramayan* and the *Mahabharat* as "Rummy-aana" and "Mahaa-bharaataa!"

Quite unlike some of the other flighty teachers, Miss Bartlett seemed destined to join the ranks of spinsters and was never ever seen with makeup or a male admirer. I think the only cosmetic aid she ever used was a powder puff. I also sometimes wondered whether she smoked in the privacy of her quarters. Miss Jansen, an Indo-German lady who taught me in the First and Second Standard, on the other hand, was almost military-like in her bearing and stride. And, she smoked (of course, never in class!) with an outrageous flair. Her hair was always braided into two plaits that were then looped over each other and pinned on top of her head. She always wore hoop earrings and a very vivid red lipstick. And, she didn't laugh... she cackled, like a witch!

The year ended with the usual Nativity play followed by a grand bonfire of pinecones and trunks of Deodar wood in the sports ground in front of our class. We also threw all the year's notebooks and books into the bonfire and watched them burn merrily, singing the blasphemous "No more Hindi, no more French, no more sitting on the classroom bench..." It didn't matter that we were not taught French in junior school. The singsong chant ended with, "And if the teacher interferes, knock her down and box her ears!"

---

4 The common Myna or Indian Myna, sometimes spelled Mynah, is a member of the Sturnidae family native to Asia.

Chapter 13

Saffron Summers

An outbreak of the tiny, yellow, star-like flowers would be the first sign of thaw in the cold weather. They also reminded us that schools would be opening in another week or two, so school uniforms would be kept washed, ironed and ready. Shoes that had been gathering mildew were cleaned and polished. I would always pluck the first yellow flowers I saw and, holding them in my cupped palms, would bring them home to show to my mother. Soon, the apricot and apple trees would burst in a glorious profusion of white and pink blossoms. As the days grew warmer, she would pull out the bulbs of Dahlias and Gladioli that had been dug up and kept in the storeroom during the winter, and the chowkidar would be told to get fresh manure and replant them in the flowerbeds around the house. I would lend a helping hand by digging up the old compressed mud and manure with a *daraanti*[1], while the chowkidar would spread out the manure in the flowerbeds. This would now be left for a few days to settle down, after which my mother would decide which bulbs to plant where.

The next flowers to bloom would be the two-tone, buttonhole marigolds that were usually deep red and yellow. These were

---

[1] A small pickaxe.

highly coveted by my grandmother who would pluck them off as soon as they bloomed and offer them to the gods during her morning prayers. When the larger, yellower marigolds were in full bloom, that would be the time when the men in saffron robes would appear, at the head of the slope, next to our red-roofed bungalow. A band of four to five monks led by our family guru Swami Mohangiriji from the pilgrim town of Haridwar, would descend upon us every year to escape the heat and dust of the plains. Our home provided them a cool retreat for two months. Our daily schedules would be rearranged to accommodate their *aartis, kirtans, satsangs*[2] and what not. For the children, it basically meant touching the Swamiji's feet to seek his blessings before rushing off to school, then coming and touching them again when we got back home. Aarti would be held around six-thirty in the evenings, which we perforce had to attend, before stepping out for our evening jaunts into the town, to roller skate or just saunter around on the Mall with our friends.

As school remained shut on weekends, we could spend more time with Swamiji and his monks. After breakfast, we would usually go and sit around him in his room and chitchat. He would enquire how we were doing at school, what games we played, or sometimes he just sat quietly smiling while we engaged with his Man Friday, Swami Bodhgiri, a tall, lanky, jovial figure whom we found most endearing because he would talk about movies and roller skating and picnics with us. The fact that he seemed to favour our grandmother and aunt was, in my eyes, perhaps his only non-redeeming aspect. He was also the elder Swamiji's launderer and would wash his saffron robe and undergarments every morning and then, chanting something like "Hare Ram, Hare Ram" or "Shiv Shambhu, Shiv Shambhu" would, with a lightness of step, carry the bucketful of clothes out into the sun to spread them on the clothesline in the kirkit ground behind the house.

---

2 Puja rituals, religious songs, gatherings.

The colour orange would then seem to dominate the house and create an ambience of cheer, brightness... and, if I must add, holiness. This was also the time when it appeared as if my mother and grandmother had, without saying so, agreed to a truce of sorts. Instead of their usual angry, high-pitched voices and verbal onslaughts accompanied by sobs and tears – a strange, somewhat uneasy calm pervaded the house. My mother seemed to spend most of her waking hours in the kitchen cooking for a household of over twenty people. I don't recall my aunt ever lending a helping hand. She always got away by appearing to do something or the other for the Swamiji and thereafter, feigning weakness and fatigue. The fact that she didn't know how to cut vegetables or cook was beside the point. The servants were overworked, most of all poor Dharmu, the sweeper boy, who now had ton-loads of shit to clear and cart away on his head down to the septic tank I presume, but I really don't know where it all went!

Swamiji would often, along with his entourage, be invited out for lunch at various homes in Mussoorie. I had a sneaking suspicion that my grandmother and aunt would command or persuade their *baniyani* (wives of the baniyas who ran the provision and general stores) friends to host the lunch. Whatever may have been the case, it provided a big relief to my mother and the servants who could then take it easy in the kitchen that day. After his sojourn in our home got over, Swamiji would, one fine day, take the bus ride back to his ashram at Haridwar.

However, that was not the last we would be seeing of the saffron robes.

My father had a great predilection for all manner of sadhus, seers and charlatans, and any category of these visiting the hill station would invariably wind their way down to our house. They would usually forecast happier, more prosperous times and would get their due rewards in terms of cash donation, clothing and rations. The ones who foretold of adverse circumstances usually got short shrift. A couple of times, the *firangi*[3] devotees of these sadhus or Swamis would also tag along and be invited to stay at our house. Once we had this rather pretty girl among the foreign disciples staying at our house. She appeared a cheerful kind, but the next morning she was found weeping and dabbing her eyes. No one quite knew what had gone wrong. I thought maybe she got news that her father or mother had died. All she would say was that she couldn't open her eyes that were squeezed shut with pain. My father told the two men accompanying her to take her to the Community Hospital that was run by missionaries in far off Landour. There, she told the doctors that she was wearing hard contact lens and had not removed them before going to bed at night. She had been wearing them continuously for over forty-eight hours! I wouldn't know what they did, but somehow the doctors were able to remove her lens and at last she could open her eyes. Stupid cow! She was probably too embarrassed to let anyone know that she wore contact lens!

Then there was this famished-looking, aged Swami who came with a horde of disciples and overstayed at our house. He was around seventy-five years old and wore a thin, white muslin dhoti that hid nothing and revealed everything. I can't remember ever having seen him sitting up because he was always reclining. He advised my father to conduct a massive *yagna*[4] to dispel malignant spirits and open the doors to prosperity. News travelled that Sharmaji was performing a grand yagna with tons of ghee being poured into the sacrificial fire, and almost everyone we knew, and even those we didn't, turned up to witness the grand ceremony. We all thought that now, since the Gods had been invoked and evil spirits banished from

---

3 Foreigner.
4 Fire ritual for warding off evil spirits.

the house, our family's fortunes would finally see an upswing but they just appeared to slide faster into decline.

One summer morning, a young sadhu came down the slope of the new house we had shifted into in 1964. His long, light brown hair was streaked by blond strands, bleached either by the sun or some strange herbal concoction, and coiled loosely above his head. What was remarkable about him was that his skin appeared golden and his eyes were icy blue. Wearing a saffron robe and not much else except for a *mala*[5] of *rudraksh*[6] beads, he came for a meal but stayed over for a few days.

My sister Tosh felt drawn to him and offered her room up for him to stay in. I think she was a bit infatuated by his striking good looks, just as I in those days got besotted with our bakery boy's swarthy brown skin and bright green eyes that flashed with an inner amusement! Now, I don't know whether this young sadhu saw some spark of spirituality in my sister or not, but on leaving he gave her a picture of *Shiva*[7] and *Parvati*[8] and a *mantra*[9] to recite. Very soon, she and that picture became inseparable. She would pray to it morning and night, I suspect, for a husband as handsome as the young sadhu. Later, she told us that the picture had miraculous properties and that she once saw Shiva turn his head in the picture to look directly at her, instead of at Parvati who was sitting next to him in the picture!

This reminds me of a Bengali Swami, who for some unknown reason wore a white dhoti instead of the standard saffron-coloured, and occupied the servant's quarters in a *Seth's*[10] bungalows. He was a year-round resident and come sunshine,

---

5 String of beads.
6 A large evergreen broad-leaved tree whose seed is used for prayer beads.
7 One of the Gods of the Hindu Trinity.
8 Shiva's consort.
9 Prayer verse.
10 A rich man.

rain, sleet or snow, he would walk about clad only in his white dhoti that also served to cover a part of his upper bare body. His jet black, heavily oiled hair contrasted strikingly with the white garb. He didn't at all appear spiritual to me, but my father was happy to have him around. My grandmother didn't quite approve of him either, for the simple reason that he didn't loudly chant *"Hari Om, Hari Om"* in the manner of the other sadhus, nor carried a *kamandal*[11].

However, why I remember him particularly well is that he was the first to convey through sign language (he had taken a vow of silence for a year) that my father was no more. We had just got the news that he had had a heart attack in a taxi and my mother and I were rushing in a rickshaw to the Masonic Lodge bus and taxi stand.

As our rickshaw slowed down on the Kulri slope, another bespectacled, long-haired sadhu who habitually wore black robes and whom everyone in the town thought was crazed and a tantric to boot, swung his stick at us and shouted, "I had cursed that drunken, womanizing, notorious gambler to die, and he is dead!"

I paled visibly and shuddering with horror, because he was referring to my father, glanced at my mother to see if she had heard. But even if she had, she didn't show any indication of it and just stared ahead. On reaching the bus stand, we came to know that my father had passed away. But it was a horribly macabre way to be given the news.

---

11 A portable, wooden water carrier usually carried by sadhus in their hand.

Chapter 14

The Abduction of Kisna

Fair as fresh cream, grey-green eyes, and corn-coloured hair that hung like silken strands around his head. Kisna was all of fourteen when his father, who delivered milk to our home, brought him to our house one fine morning. It was a holiday; I was playing marbles with a servant boy in the gravel patch outside the kitchen. My mother came out of the kitchen with a vessel to take the milk and stopped short. "*Memsahib*," said Bhimsingh, "*Yeh mera beta hai Kisna,*"[1] and then turning to the boy prodded him to touch my mother's feet. "*Jug-jug jiyo beta,*" my mother stroked the boy's head in a blessing. "*Bhimsingh tum baitho, mein isske liye chai aur biscuit laati hoon,*"[2] she said as she retreated into the kitchen and came bearing two glasses of tea and some biscuits on a steel plate. She then took a *moodha*[3] and sat down next to the visitors, while Kisna and his father politely sipped tea. I came and took a biscuit off their plate to munch.

"*Memsahib,*" started Kisna's father, "*Maine suna hai aapke yahan ek mahaan sadhu thehre huey hain. Mujhe Kisna ko unhe*

---

[1] Memsahib, this is my son Kisna.
[2] May you live long, son. Bhimsingh, you wait while I get some tea and biscuits for the boy.
[3] Small cane stool.

dikhaana hai... yeh picchley chhe mahiney se na kuch bolta hai, na khelta hai. Isski maa ne issko school se bhi nikaal liya hai."[4] All this, while Kisna appeared to be blissfully unaware that he was the subject of discussion and kept eating biscuits and sipping his tea quietly. I was intrigued, and to elicit some response from him invited him to play marbles with us, but he did not pay heed to what I said.

What was the problem with Kisna? Here is the gist of what his father told my mother that morning:

There is a hillock called Pari Tibba in Mussoorie. It is about five or six kilometres from our house, in the direction of Landour, from where a side road leads down towards a forest path to Kisna's village beyond Mossy Falls. To reach that village one has to cross Pari Tibba. A year ago, I had gone for a day's summer outing with my friend Dharampal. The rough, narrow path, which we call a *pagdandi*, cuts through a dense forest, laden with all kinds of trees – pine, oak, rhododendron and others.

Cowherds and goatherds usually come there to graze their livestock. Sometimes one can hear a faint musical tinkle of bells worn around the neck of livestock, as they munch contentedly on the grass or shrubbery along the hill slopes. What I found most odd about Pari Tibba was that, in the midst of all that greenery, there was a fairly wide patch where the grass golden and soft as cornsilk. I did mention this to my friend and half-jokingly noted that this was probably the place where fairies came out to dance under the silvery light of a full moon.

"*Mazaak mat kar Gattu, nahin toh pariyan tere ko bhi le jaayengi,*"[5] he said in a serious tone.

---

[4] I heard that a great sadhu is staying at your house. I want him to see Kisna. My son hasn't spoken a word since six months, nor does he play with other boys. His mother has had to take him out of school.

[5] Don't make fun Gattu, or the fairies will take you.

The Hill Billy

"*Pariyan? Hai, kaash mujhe bhi le jayen,*"[6] I said with mock enthusiasm. Then to tease him further, I added, "*Sun-sun, ghungruon ki awaaz sunaayi di? Aisa lagata hain ki do pariyan idhar aa rahi hain.*"[7]

He landed me one playful cuff in answer and we walked on.

Getting back to Bhimsingh, he said that Kisna often went to graze his goats on Pari Tibba. He would leave in the morning and come home well before sun set. His mother would pack a few *rotis*[8], pickle, and dry *subzi*[9], for his midday meal and hand it to him along with his flute, which he always carried tucked in a cloth pouch tied to his waist. It's a well-known fact that cows and goats give more milk when they hear music, and Kisna was quite adept at playing his flute.

One evening, Kisna did not come home. His mother waited well past sunset. Another youth from the village found the goats making their way home and, not able to spot Kisna anywhere, herded them down to the village. When Kisna's father Bhimsingh returned, he found his wife distraught. She was being consoled and comforted by the womenfolk.

"Bhima, O Bhima," informed one of the village elders, "Kisna is missing... he hasn't come home... we have asked his friends but no one seems to have seen him today..." Bhima set down the empty cans of milk he was carrying and went to his wife. "You should have sent his Uncle to go look for him!" His wife, Champa, turned tearfully to him and half-sobbed, "He went to Dehradun this morning and will likely return tomorrow." "Who will come with me to look for the boy?" asked Bhima, turning to look around at the menfolk of the village.

---

6 Fairies? I wish they would take me also.

7 Listen-listen, do you hear the sound of ghungroos? I think that two fairies are coming towards us.

8 Flat, round, Indian bread made of unleavened flour.

9 A spicy, vegetable preparation.

Several voices spoke out at once.

"At this time of the night? Where will we look for him?"

"What if he has fallen into some *khud*[10]?"

"There are no leopards or panthers on Pari Tibba... just some wild hares and silver fox. They would pose no danger to the boy."

"Maybe not animals, but what about the parees?" intoned an old woman. At this pronouncement, an ominous silence descended on the gathering. They appeared to be holding their collective breath. Not a cow mooed, nor a lamb bleated.

Most residents of Mussoorie were not even aware of a place called Pari Tibba that literally translates as 'Fairy Hill'. Even if they were, they dismissed it as a whimsical name given by the superstitious villagers. Yet, there were rumours and half-baked stories about Pari Tibba doing the round of the surrounding villages.

"Fairies? *Fai-r-r-r-ies!*" you may ask incredulously. This is the twentieth century and you talk of fairies? Well, why not? If you can believe in aliens from outer space, in ghosts that walk the lonely paths at night, in demonic possession and haunted houses – then why do you scoff and disbelieve in fairies? Anyways, continuing with his story, Bhimsingh told my mother that a few lads from the village accompanied him that night with lanterns and torches to look for his son. "*Kisna... Kisna... Kisna,*" they yelled, the mythological name echoing in the hills. Kisna didn't answer. They did not find him. A 'missing person' report was lodged at the Landour Police Station, later that night. The police sent a search party to comb the hill, but they didn't turn up anything. Not a piece of clothing, nor the remnants of his lunch, nor his flute.

One week later, just before sunset, Kisna suddenly turned up at the door of his house. The village women followed him, whispering among themselves in hushed tones. His once black

---

10 Ravine.

hair was now burnished gold. His eyes stared vacantly. He had, so it appeared, been struck mute. His mother, shocked but overjoyed to have him back, hugged, coaxed and cajoled him, but Kisna didn't utter a sound.

"We don't know what happened to Kisna or where he was for the entire week. He has been like this for over six months now, Memsahib. He doesn't play with the other children, he doesn't recognise his friends; I don't even know if he recognizes us as his parents. He doesn't even play his flute anymore! Please ask the sadhu baba if he can do something."

It was time for the morning aarti so my mother asked them to follow her to the sadhu baba's room. Kisna quietly followed them in. My mother briefly told sadhu baba the story about Kisna's mysterious disappearance. Upon hearing the story, the ascetic called the boy to him and putting his hand on his head, gave him a coconut and some flowers. "The boy has been touched," is all he said cryptically.

So, what happened to Kisna?

Had the fairies taken him for their pleasure and then sent him back? Haven't we heard or read enough about fairies and wood nymphs being smitten by beautiful young boys and luring them with their wiles? Who isn't familiar with the story of Venus and Adonis?

Had Kisna fallen off somewhere, lost his memory and his voice, and then wandered back to his village? Had he seen something, which he wasn't meant to see, and therefore had his memory erased?

A year has gone by. The light in Kisna's eyes has not returned. Neither has his voice.

I sometimes wonder what happened to Kisna that night of the full moon. What do you think?

As for me, I never went back to Pari Tibba again.

Chapter 15

The Student and The Star

Lying in the cans for over five years, she burst upon the silver screen almost overnight. Short, nubile, all of eighteen, but with a bosom as full as the wind-filled sails of a schooner on the high seas, and hips that swivelled like a grinding wheel. Ever the coquette, she had a sparkling merriment in her eyes and black, moist, glossy lips that always remained slightly parted even when they were shut. She looked straight into my eyes from full-page ads in *Screen* – then, the leading film weekly, black and white like the Bollywood films of the late 1950s and the early 60s.

I was twelve, bursting with testosterone and totally smitten. Her face would haunt my dreams during the night and beguile me during the day, when I would leaf through magazines at the local bookshops. The film was still a month away from release in the nearest town that was Dehradun, the cinema halls of Mussoorie having already downed their shutters for the winter. Its songs, aired on AIR's (All India Radio) *Vividh Bharati* and *Radio Ceylon*, were already foot-tapping hits.

For some reason that I now can't recall, my mother, middle sister Santosh, and I were in Delhi during December of that year. So also was a distant cousin of ours. The movie had just been released at Odeon theatre and I pestered my cousin that I had to see it or else I would die. I begged him to get our mother's permission, for she would never let my sister and I go by ourselves, as we were too young to be gallivanting around Delhi alone.

At first, he refused outright saying that, "I don't want to waste my money seeing some stupid new actress in a movie no one has heard of! Besides she looks quite ordinary to me!" Now, I couldn't bear such an affront to my heart-throb and gave him a solid punch in his stomach.

"Owww!" he howled, "What was that for?"

"That was for calling her stupid and ordinary. She's the most beautiful creature I have laid eyes on!"

"Hahahaha," he clutched his stomach and laughed and did a jig. "You milk-drinking baby, first grow a fuzz over your lip and then drool over girls!"

He was barely seventeen and considered himself a handsome young stud. I cajoled, coaxed, and begged. Nothing seemed to work. Then I stooped to downright blackmail. I said, "Okay, if you won't take me, I will tell my mother *and* your mother about that time when you were doing hanky-panky with the maidservant." That was enough of a threat to make him do a double-take and give in to my demand. But he didn't without exacting a promise from me. "You will have to do something... whatever I ask, whenever I ask... for me." I promised, "Anything!"

The next day found the three of us outside Odeon theatre among the crowd waiting for the first show to get over, and the doors to open before we could get in.

Those were the days when the feature film would be preceded by the tedious Indian News Review documentary that was followed by advertisements for various products. When the Censor certificate for the feature flashed on screen, my fists clenched, my knees locked and, seated in the third row from the screen, I caught my breath. The movie credits began to roll to the refrain of the instrumental version of the theme song of the movie. Then, she came, she cavorted and she conquered. I was delirious. I was smiling from ear to ear when we stepped out in the intermission for some eats and drinks. In the theatre, people whistled and threw coins at the screen when the penultimate song and dance number, a hybrid blend of rock-n-roll and Punjabi *Bhangra*[1], rocked the screen.

I was no longer just infatuated. I was in love. She tormented me in my dreams, and in my waking hours. I could think of nothing but her. My best friend, a boy twelve years older, egged me on to write her a letter and the day I got a reply, I couldn't open the envelope for hours – delaying and savouring the moments of holding and shuffling it in my moist palms. At last, in the privacy of my bedroom, I slit the envelope open and an autographed photograph of the star slipped out. The letter written in her hand was read and re-read a dozen times every day over the next few days, and I slept with it tucked under my pillow at night. My parents, who were well aware of what was going on, decided to good-naturedly go along with my adolescent love affair.

At the skating rink, I would put on my roller skates but would sit lovelorn at the tables lined along the floor and gaze out of the glazed windows of the in-house restaurant that overlooked the Doon valley. My friend Dharmpal would often join me there in the evening. He egged me on to write another letter to the film heroine, imploring her to visit Mussoorie. But was there any hope of that happening? Not a chance! All the same, I would imagine her driving up in a red car along the road that zigzagged up to our little hill station. Call it the power of thought, influencing events or call it sheer coincidence, but one day my friend rang up to announce, "Gattu[2], I have great news for you! Come down

[1] A vigorous form of dance from the northern plains of Punjab.
[2] Gattu was my pet name.

now to Barretto's shop and I will tell you. Come fast!"

I pulled on my boots and ran down the shortcut and arrived out of breath at Barretto's shop. Dharmpal, of the twinkling eyes and heavily-oiled black hair, was showing all his sparkling thirty-two and hugged me as I came up to him. "*Arrey Gattu, bahut khushkhabri hai... teri woh heroine aaj Charleville Hotel mein aa kar thehri hai. Usske saath ek kaala marwari seth bhi hai!*"[3] "*Tu sach bol raha hai kya?*" I exclaimed, "*Mujhe ullu toh nahi bana raha?*"[4] I was beside myself with joy. God had heard my prayers and sent her to me. I rushed back home to tell my father (who was as filmi as they come) and insisted he call up the owner of Charleville Hotel and arrange a meeting for us with the nubile star. And, it was that easily done. We had an appointment to meet her at 11 am the next day!

My father wore his favourite grey achkan and snowwhite salwar, and I wore my favourite sleeveless, leopard-print sweater over a pale yellow shirt and off we went to Charleville Hotel. The owner of the hotel came to greet my father and said, "*Kyun Sharmaji, iss umar mein aapko actresses ka shauq chada hai, bhabhi kya kehti hain?*"[5] My father laughed and said, "*Nahin, nahin Lalaji, mein nahi, mere puttar par usska bhoot sawaar hai!*"[6] I blushed a dozen shades of pink as he led us up the stairway towards her suite and knocked on the door. The dark-complexioned Seth opened the door and ushered the hotel owner and us in. As we sat down on stiff, horse-hair stuffed ornate chairs, he said, "She is getting ready and will be out in a minute," then turned his face towards the bedroom door and announced, "Madam, your guests have come!"

---

[3] Gattu, there's thrilling news... your film heroine has come to Charleville Hotel accompanied by a rich, dark marwari man.

[4] Are you telling the truth... you are not making an owl out of me are you?

[5] Why Mr. Sharma, at this age you are running after actresses now... what does your wife have to say?'

[6] No, no, it's not me but my son here who is mad after her.

She traipsed in wearing tight, form-fitting slacks and a flouncy top. Her hair fell in curls around her oval face and she looked even more beautiful than she did in black-and-white on screen. Flashing a bright smile she did a namaste to my father, and turning to me she said, "So, you are the boy who has been writing those nice letters to me!" I blushed, I stammered and I stuttered "Yy-y-e-sss." She said, "They are so sweet, I even showed them to my mother."

The Seth and the actress were then ready for a visit to the Botanical Gardens of Mussoorie and said they would be happy if we accompanied them. So, while she got on a pony, the rest of us walked either alongside or behind her. How I wished I could hold the horse's bridle instead of the horseman. At the gardens, we took a few pictures and then she exclaimed she was tired and wanted to get back to the hotel. We invited her and her companion for tea to our house but for some reason that didn't materialise. However, we did run into her again on the Mall Road, the next evening. She and the Seth were riding a rickshaw and stopped a minute to say 'Hi-hello'. They were leaving the next morning for Bombay but she extracted a promise from me that I would keep writing to her.

The day she left, my friend rang up excitedly asking me to run down and meet him near the Charleville post office. He said he had something special to show me. When I landed up at the post office, he was nowhere around and I asked the postman if Dharmpal had been around. He said, "Yes", and that I should wait for him to return. I walked around the hotel staring up at the balcony of the suite she had been occupying, hoping against hope that she would make an appearance. She didn't, but I felt a tap on my shoulder and my friend whispered, "Come, I have something for you, but I can't show it to you here. Let's walk further down to the gate." I was impatient and asked him to show what he wanted to. He pulled out an envelope and said he had filched it from the postman when he was clearing the mail. My heartthrob who was staying at the hotel had personally told the postman that it must be sent in the first clearance that day. My friend had bribed the postman with five rupees to hand over the envelope to him. With trembling hands and sweaty fingers, I opened the envelope that had been imprinted with a lipstick mark.

Written in a school-girlish handwriting on ruled paper, I still remember snatches from that pale blue letterhead. It started off with "My darling," and went on to say, "I am here... but my heart is there with you. The Seth is a tiresome fellow, I hate being with him," and then a few lines later it read, "My nipples are still hurting from the time you pinched them before I left... they want to feel the touch of your fingers again... I am coming soon to you."

I was close to tears by the time I finished reading the letter. My friend begged, *"Kissi ko mat bataana maine yeh tere liye kiya hai, I will be thrown in jail."*[7] I promised him I wouldn't tell anyone and stuffed the envelope in my pocket and ran back home. That letter stayed with me for a couple of years till one day, rummaging through my box, I came across it and read it again, before lighting a match to it. I remembered how I used to dream of marrying her, she having my baby... all that stupid nonsense... and then I had such a good laugh over it.

Over the years, I saw all her movies – didn't miss out on a single one. In the last movie I saw, she had grown quite plump and heavy around the hips but her face remained unchanged. I followed her affairs with the male stars in the issues of *Filmfare* and *Star-n-Style*, two monthly film glossies. And then, when I had moved to Bombay and one day I walked into Gazebo's Chinese Restaurant on Hill Road, I saw her sitting at a table nearby with a woman companion. She was smoking a cigarette

---

[7] Don't tell anyone about this, or I will be thrown into jail. I have done this only for you.

and gesticulating in an exaggerated filmi manner with her long, scarlet nails that matched the shade of the lipstick she had smeared on her lips. She snapped her fingers at the waiter and said rather loudly, "*Do paan lagwa kar lao, aur chhey number ka kimam dalvana.*"[8] She was long finished as an actress; her short-lived career over in what seemed the blink of any eye, although it had been a good ten years.

Ahhhh... for dreams of fair women! But, 'age *had* withered and custom staled her infinite variety'[9] of *nakhras*[10] and mannerisms that now appeared embarrassingly ludicrous. Once a star... and now a harridan. The pity of it!

---

8   Bring two paans with six number tobacco flavour.

9   With apologies to Shakespeare.

10 Coquette.

Chapter 16

Walking Shoes, Knocking Knees

I have always been resistant to change. Change of schools. Change of classrooms. Change of teachers. Change of residence. Change of walking shoes, too! New shoes always tend to squeeze, pinch, cut and bruise the heels and toes until they get broken in. But change is, and has been, the one constant throughout – sometimes for the better, and sometimes for the best. But more of changing tracks, later. For now, it meant a brand new pair of walking shoes.

During a specially convened school assembly one morning, our Principal, the tall and gangly Pastor Manley of the Seventh Day Adventist Vincent Hill School, cheerfully announced that the school was organising its annual one-week trek to Nag Tibba (Snake Hill) seven days later. I had barely been six months at this school, and I shuddered in my shoes at the thought of remaining away from home for not a day or two, but one whole week! I quivered and quaked all the way home after school that particular day. I was sullen and sulky, and told my father to tell the Princy that I was frail and sick and couldn't go on the strenuous hike. He tried, but the Princy said it was compulsory for all students to attend the event and no exceptions could be made – not even for the only Indian boy in a school filled with white Americans of a particular missionary order.

My father had been so proud when he had me admitted to this all-white, all-American school for boys and girls. He was proud of the fact that I was the only Indian student they had accepted. I had been shown visions of going to college in America after graduating from High School. Of course, at that time, I was completely clueless where America was and why one should aspire to go there for higher studies. No one knew what a disadvantage it would later turn out to be.

The next day, the class teacher handed out a list of things that had to be brought along for the hike. The two most important items were a sturdy rucksack and a pair of stout walking shoes. The rucksack that weighed almost five kilos empty was found in a store that sold antique furniture and some World War II memorabilia. It apparently belonged to one of the British or Aussie soldiers from the Mussoorie cantonment. It covered almost my entire back but could hold a roll of blanket, a week's clothing, towels, and the works! The shoes were another matter, more difficult to find because those weren't the days of Nike and Adidas. I had to therefore settle for a pair of Bata's keds that really didn't qualify as stout or sturdy. I could even feel small pebbles poke through the soles.

I was to join the hikers at a pre-determined central spot in town at the unearthly hour of 6 am. My servant, who was carrying the rucksack on his back, accompanied me to the meeting point. There, they were already gabbing and giggling away – an advance group of blue-jeaned boys and skirted girls (girls were forbidden to wear jeans and tees!). As we started on the first lap of our trek, my class teacher asked, "Hey Shiv! You can't bring this servant boy with you!" Bewildered, I asked, "Why not? Who would carry my heavy rucksack with the blanket roll and pillow?"

The teacher rolled up his eyes, clapped his hands and

shouted out, "Hey guys, this Indy boy wants to bring his servant along to carry his rucksack! Ain't that rich!! Haw-haw-haw..." and everyone joined in his caw-caw. He then came to me and said, "Come on, swing the rucksack around your shoulders and strap it up!" I almost doubled over with its weight and if he hadn't caught me, I would have fallen flat on my face on the road. Anyway, I soon got the hang of it and trudged along, among the last boys trailing the trekkers. I took a backward glance to see my servant boy who was standing there grinning like a donkey! I cringed at the story he would go and tell my parents back home.

When the trekking party reached the midway point to Nag Tibba, Mr. Hooper, one of the trek leaders blew a shrill blast on his whistle and, holding up a newspaper rolled up to serve as a makeshift megaphone, he told us to break into groups of ten each, before we stepped onto the bridge. When the first group had crossed over the bridge that was at least sixty feet across the Shukrayani River, the group leader waved a scarf, and would then again wave it from the other end for the next group to cross over.

The first day of the hike went off rather smoothly with the usual pitching of tents – boys' tents separated from the girls' by two terraced fields. Bobby, the Princy's son, a rotund little boy, had been cajoled and coaxed by his parents, no doubt, to tent up with me. I must say he put quite a good face on it and didn't let on that he had been instructed to invite me to tent with him. He was a cheery, red-faced boy with a high-pitched, squeaky voice. I had secretly wanted to tent with Buddy who was also my classmate, and was always nice to me in class unlike some of the other hooligans.

Buddy was also handsome in the '50s style with his blond hair wet, parted, puffed, and plastered down sideways. And he had the most awesome bow-shaped, deep pink, pouting lips and a pair of the brightest blue eyes I had ever seen. No, I didn't have a crush on Buddy Smith but I liked him. And after two nights out in the pinewood forest, my secret desire got fulfilled. Buddy asked if I would like to share his tent with him, and I replied, "Let's go check with Bobby." Bobby, the happy-go-lucky lad that he was said, "Sure guys, you two go ahead, I will shack up with myself."

It was the month of July, when it usually rained heavily in the hills. In the middle of the night, the heavens opened their bowels and let loose their pent-up heat and dust in a raging downpour. The roll of thunder echoed in the hills, lightning flashed and streaked, lighting up the gigantic, swaying branches of the pine trees. Rain pelted down on our makeshift tent of sheer canvas strung across a rope tied between two trees. While setting up the tents, everyone had dug a narrow trench around them as a precaution against the rain, but this was no passing shower.

As it started dripping down on us through the thin canvas sheet, Buddy said, "Hurry up Shiv, let's rush out and grab your canvas holdall. We will throw it over the tent. That way, the water won't come in!" "But Buddy, where will I sleep?" I protested. He laughed, "Come on, you are skinny enough to slip into my sleeping bag with me." We dashed out and swung the holdall over and across the tent. While I held a flashlight, Buddy quickly tried to deepen the trench with a stout twig of a branch that he found behind our tent. Then we both scrambled inside, our wet Tees sticking to us. "Shuck off that tee and put this on," he said, shoving a crumpled bundle towards me. He then yanked off his wet shirt and threw it in a corner of the tent. I caught my breath as a flash of lightning lit up his bare, hairless torso – white, smooth, pink-nippled and taut! I pulled out my face towel and quickly rubbed his back and then towelled his wet hair, while he snatched another T-shirt out of his rucksack and pulled it over himself.

He unzipped the other side of the sleeping bag and told me to slide in. It was a tight squeeze and we huddled spoon-like, shivering for a while until the warmth of each other's bodies calmed the trembling. I fell asleep like that, with my arms wrapped around Buddy's chest from behind.

The days appeared to fly with sneaking off for fishing excursions that were forbidden, rounds of baseball and volleyball, barbecue and bonfire nights. However, the night before we were to leave, the bowels of the sky opened again and unleashed one of the heaviest downpours of the season. Caught totally off-guard, everyone scrambled towards the *Dak Bungalow*, as the Forest Ranger's office-cum-residence was known. And that was the only night I think they were left with no choice but to let the girls and boys sleep under one roof, with just some sheets spread on a string to provide a semblance of privacy. The next morning, everything was in a mess – wet blankets, wet shoes, and wet bread. However, the sun was shining bright and our departure was put off by a day to allow everything to dry out in the sun.

A day later, after a frugal breakfast of rotis, pickle, onions, and fried potatoes bought from the nearby village, we began the trek back to school. All of us were in high spirits – the girls were humming songs, while the boys were generally horsing around. Around noon, the track wound itself up and around a hill and forked out. One track now led to a village on the other hill, and the other led us towards the bridge that we had to cross to get over to the other side. A few boys went ahead as an advance party, while Buddy and I lagged behind with the rest of the troupe.

Suddenly, Martin, one of the boys who had gone on ahead came running back towards us.

"Hey guys!" He huffed out of breath. "You should see that bridge – man, it's been knocked out by the downpour.

Sheee-ssh..! Old Hooper has got his balls in a twist and is
checking the bridge out with Jim and Wesley. If it's uncrossable,
then guess what! We will all have to roll up our jeans and
wade through the river. Ohh-hh man... what with those big
slippery rocks, it's gonna be some damn crossing!"

Hooper sent a scout back who said that the old man had
instructed that the girls would be the first to cross and we were to
wait for a blast from his whistle to be the next group to move.

"Pheeeee...pheeeee," sounded Hooper's whistle signalling
that the first gaggle of girls should move forward. Plump Patsy
led the group with a cheerful, "C'mon girls, let's rock the
bridge!" Hooper's face went red as a beetroot as he shouted,
"Pattt-sssy... you rock that bridge and you will end up cracking
your skull on the rocks below!" The rest of us huddled near the
bridge. The first batch was taken across by a senior boy leading
at the front and another bringing up the rear. Hooper on his
makeshift megaphone yelled, "Take it slow and easy, girls."
Then he turned towards us to select the next group that would
go on the bridge. And so on it went, until all but the last group
of seven boys remained to cross over. Among them was our
school's only Indonesian boy, a surprisingly tall six-footer called
Tom. Those who had already reached the other side were told
not to crowd the bridge but to press on ahead.

The downpour had loosened a plank on the bridge that
was roughly forty to fifty feet high above the river and we had
been told to keep our eyes peeled while we crossed. Tom was
bringing up the rear of the last column of boys. Having taken
the footfalls of at least eighty to ninety students who had earlier
crossed over, the bridge was now swaying a little precariously.
Tom's foot caught in a loosened plank and the swaying bridge
caused him to lose his balance. His hands stretched out to grasp
the ropes that rang alongside but with a frightening scream he
toppled and fell headlong from the bridge into the river below.

Hooper, who was leading the boys yelled, "Don't stop! Don't look down! Keep walking slowly to the end of the bridge." Once across, the boys rushed into mid-stream along with Hooper. Tom was lying arched on his back on the rocks, his eyes wide open – unconscious and bleeding from a crack in his skull. One of the senior boys was sent as a runner to go and call our Principal, who had gone on ahead with the first group of students. Numbed with shock, the boys under Hooper's directions quickly made a stretcher out of some thick bamboos growing along the banks of the river.

Tom was carefully lifted and placed on the stretcher that the boys carried for fifteen miles to the closest hospital in Landour. A pall of gloom had fallen over everyone when I reached school the next day. Tom, it was rumoured, had cracked his spine and was lying comatose in a room of the Community Hospital. Hooper and a few other boys were still camped there. Tom's parents had been informed of the accident and they had caught the earliest flight out of Java. Taking a cab from Delhi, they had driven nearly three hundred and seventy-odd miles to reach the hospital, late at night. They never left his bedside. After five days, Tom succumbed to his injuries and passed away – without knowing that his mother and father were by his side.

Tom was buried in the cemetery at Mussoorie. A quiet service was held for him in the school chapel. Tom's father spoke briefly of his son. There was no blame placed on anyone for the tragic accident. Rather, he made special mention of the boys who had carried Tom on the stretcher all the way uphill to the hospital and stayed praying by his side that night. A prayer was all that he asked from us now. A prayer to God that He accept the soul of young Tom in His loving care.

Tom's parents left the next day. We were left with memories of a boy who always had a ready smile for everyone. Yet, as it happens with memories, these also faded away before the school year was out.

Was I happy at school? Not really. But all said and done, I wasn't miserable either. Yes, I learned to play baseball and volleyball but was always the last person to be picked by the opposing teams. It was as if they *had to* take me else the sports master would compel them to do it. I can't really blame anyone, because I never really made any effort to be good at either sport. Even in the school gym, that was compulsory to attend, I would hide behind other boys so the gym instructor, a strikingly tall, young man, would not pick on me and make me jump over the 'wooden horse'. I don't think we exchanged much more than a "Hi-hello" during my eight years there.

We were a class of three students in my graduation year. There was Joyce, the girl with slant eyes and pouting lips whom all the boys wanted to be linked with, and there was Danetta who was on steel crutches because of a polio attack she had suffered and endured during our eighth grade, and there was I. We were graduating from High School and preparations for the ceremony were on. One of us had to be elected President and since I was the only boy around, the teacher insisted I don the mantle.

Now, being appointed the President meant that I would have to make a speech in front of the whole school – a prospect that quite unnerved me. So I suggested that why not make one of the girls the President, a suggestion that was mocked and ridiculed because the teacher said the President was always a male and I, hopefully, was man enough to take on the job. "Or, was he to assume I was a wimp?" he jibed. There was just no getting out of this predicament. Well, to cut a sad story short, there I was on our graduation night, standing in the wings, my hands already trembling and my sweaty palms clutching at a sheet of paper with the speech that I was to deliver. They had even removed the lectern and I stood, feeling totally naked, in front of the whole assembly. It was mid-November, cold as a witch's tit, and I was wearing a suit and sweating as if it was midsummer. Joyce and Danetta stood in the wings, grinning at my plight.

How I stuttered and stammered my way through the speech I don't know, but it seemed it was over before it had begun, and there was a smattering of polite applause. I bowed and made a hurried exit.

But that was not the only embarassing thing about my graduation day. There was another, even more shameful act that I had earlier perpetrated. The Principal had told me that I must invite my parents for the ceremony. Now, I knew my father would come wearing his salwar and achkan and those golden, embroidered, upturned nawabi footwear, and that my mother, even though she was a very beautiful woman, would come in her silk sari, with her hair plaited into a *jalebi jooda*[1] and wearing her heaviest gold finery. So, I did a really despicable thing. I told the Principal that my father was away in Delhi on some business and my mother could not come alone at that late hour in the evening. And, I never told my parents about his invitation. I was ashamed how they would look among the white Americans. And I have remained ashamed of my shameful act of having dishonoured my parents in thought, word and deed that night. King Lear rightly moaned, "Sharper than a serpent's tooth is the ingratitude of a child..."

The evening ended with the annual *Burrakhana*, which literally translates as the Big Dinner. This was my last night at the school to which I would never return. But like a prisoner gets attached to the walls and bars of his cell over a long confinement, I had a lump in my throat as I slowly climbed up the path with its raised concrete breakers to keep the gravel in place, and walked under and out the concrete arch that proclaimed the legend 'Vincent Hill High School'.

The cold, bleak winter had begun to set in.

---

[1] Hair coiled into a spiral bun.

Chapter 17

Of Ping-Pong and Other Balls

I may have failed to mention that our father had a remarkably flourishing business in the manufacture of sports goods in Sialkot. Having taken over the reins of the business when my grandfather died in the autumn of 1942, he had become a millionaire at the young age of twenty-two by making cricket bats, hockey sticks and footballs that he supplied to the British.

In return, he was issued import licenses for ping-pong balls and some surgical threads and instruments that were not manufactured in India at that time. Since we had fled from Pakistan in a borrowed car in the middle of the night, "With just the clothes on our backs," as my mother was fond of saying, there was no question of packing in other valuables and lugging a truckload of cricket bats or hockey sticks as well! Strangely enough, our father had by some freak of chance managed to carry his portable Remington typewriter with him.

One afternoon, seven years later, he got a call from the Railway Office in Mussoorie that a consignment of three gunny sacks had arrived for him and would he please have it picked up. While Mussoorie was not connected by rail, it did have a railway office to which Prem was promptly dispatched on my bicycle to collect the sacks full of goodies. While we speculated what they could possibly contain, my mother said it must be the gramophone and perhaps the jewellery she had left behind... my father said they must be containing his office files and documents. After a couple of hours, Prem came wheeling the bicycle down the slope followed by a coolie who carried three bulging gunny sacks on his back.

As we kids gathered around excitedly, Prem, grinning from ear to ear, told my father, *"Bauji, vekho haramiyan ne ki pejaya veh."*[1] He was referring to the workers at the sports manufacturing unit in Sialkot, now in Pakistan. Peeping from the split seams of the sacks were small white balls. My father picked up a 7 o'clock razor blade and slashed through the brown *sutli* – a thin rope that had been used to stitch up the sacks. Out tumbled the tiny balls, most of them dented and yellowed with age. Our mother remarked, *"Lai, aida ki faida!"*[2] We, of course, were delighted and began pestering father to get us some table tennis bats from the market that very evening. Loving and generous as he always was, he not only got the bats, he brought home the whole ping-pong table with the strip of net dividing it into half.

Now the question that plagued my father's mind was what to do with sacks full of dented and yellowing ping-pong balls. After days of pondering, Paayi, the shrewd sardar, came up with the solution. He said that even in Sialkot, when balls stored over some time started yellowing, they would rub French chalk, a white imported powder, into them and allow the balls to absorb it for a few days. Then, lo and behold, the balls would turn snow white again. But first the dents had to be removed. The solution to this was fairly simple: one had to soak the balls for a couple of days in buckets of hot water and then spread them out to dry in the sun. Not a dimple would appear in the balls after that.

---

[1] Bauji, see what the bastards have sent.
[2] What's the use of these?

Since many hands were needed when it came to rubbing the balls with French chalk, my sisters and I were also roped in. Sitting on the porch, each of us would be given a folded out newspaper with a heap of white powder and told to keep on rubbing the balls with it till the yellow faded and the balls looked white as new. So successful was this operation that our father managed to sell off the entire consignment of ping-pong balls, albeit at a certain discount.

When I was in Standard Four, I got to handle other kinds of balls.

Have I mentioned that my primary education was at a girls' school that allowed boys to study only up to the Second Standard? Since I and the other two boys were meeker than the girls, we had to learn to knit and even do needlework so we could stitch on our buttons, along with the girls in our class. I told my mother that we had been asked to bring a pair of knitting needles and a ball of wool to class the next day. There, Miss Bartlett taught us to knit and purl. During that period, all we could see was pairs of hands laboriously looping the wool over and around the knitting needles to knit stitch after stitch, and all that we heard was the clickety-click of the needles. This was often punctuated with the clicking of Miss Bartlett's teeth, which she would tap against each other when she went down rows between the desks to see how everyone was progressing. Our efforts produced colourful woollen scarves, some of which had holes where stitches had been dropped by clumsy hands.

That wasn't the end of our descent into 'girliness'. We next had to tackle skeins of thread, sewing needles, circular wooden frames and a piece of cloth on which we would be taught to do needlework. The benefit of those needlework lessons back then shows up today in the buttons that I can deftly stitch back when they drop off my pants or shirts.

Years later, I would be rolling up big balls of Edam and

Cheddar cheese in my hands. Those days our father had begun doing social service. To satisfy his yearning, he became a distributor for CARE, a charitable organisation of Australia that sent cans of powdered milk, maple syrup and balls of cheese to be distributed among the poor of third-world countries. A room in the bungalow was dedicated to storing tins of milk, maple syrup, margarine and cheese balls.

He set aside two days in the week when he would distribute the goodies. The news spread and soon queues began forming, winding all the way down the slope that led towards our house and to the desk in the kirkit compound where my father sat with a register, pen and an ink pad. Two servants stood to his left and right, much like the angels Michael and Gabriel do beside God. The person at the head of the queue would move up, announce his name, number of family members and address, which my father would dutifully jot down in his register. Then he would ask, "*Doodh ya Makkhan ya Cheese?*" That is to say, "Milk or Butter or Cheese?" The recipient would invariably ask for all three even though he didn't have any clue to what cheese was, leave alone margarine.

My father would be quite disturbed when my mother or one of his own children would ask for a tin of milk, margarine or a ball of cheese. We really didn't know what to do with the maple syrup and I'm sure neither did the people who took it away with them since they were getting it free. He would say this was meant only for the poor people and it was against his conscience to divert some tins for personal use by the family. That didn't disturb us too much. We let him keep his conscience, and filched as many tins as we wanted anyway by bullying the servants. The powdered milk made excellent barfi, the margarine came in very handy while baking a cake, and the cheese was excellent for making and frying cheese balls or cheese pakodas.

My dad built this image of 'provider for the poor' assiduously over the next two years and the villagers came to recognise him as their Messiah in the white kurta-salwaar. In the third year of this largesse to the hill folk, the Mussoorie Municipal Corporation held its election for Municipal Councillors. My father had all along set his eyes upon this post and he imagined he had the villagers in the left, right and top pockets of his achkan. His main rival was the owner of a rather fancy wine shop. Canvassing began in right earnest. Voters' lists were prepared. Canvassers on both sides besmirched the characters of both the candidates. If one was a womaniser, the other was a gambler. If one was a saint, the other was a proclaimed sinner. If one balked at certain improprieties, the other shamefacedly indulged in all.

On the night before the election, while my father walked the Mall Road with his coterie shaking hands and doing namaste to every sweeper, coolie, rickshawalla, along with other night walkers, his rival was busy distributing liquor and money to voters in the villages as far off as Bhatta, Chandal Garhi and Jharipani. The ploy paid off, and the next evening when the counting of votes was over, the rival had won by a margin of around a dozen votes. My father's canvassers who had been expecting him to romp home on the strength of milk, cheese and maple syrup on which the villagers along with the poorer sections of the populace had been fattening for the past three years, were left despondent. The drummers they had organised never got to wield their drumsticks, and the garlands they wore over their wrists to drape around my father's neck should he have won, were cast aside. My father, wearing a loser's smile, walked briskly swinging his walking stick towards them and cheerily said, "*Udaas kyun hote ho, chalo ghar chalo,*"[3] and brought them all home for a last supper. If there was a Judas among his canvassers, he was never found out.

---

3 There is no reason to be sad, let's all go home.

Mussoorie had two billiard and snooker parlours – the one above Linker's was upmarket and exclusive while the other was located on the premises of the Kulri skating rink. I was introduced to billiards by a college mate who happened to be holidaying in our hills. By nature a little timid and reluctant to make a fool of myself at the tables, I resisted picking up the cue for some evenings, preferring to sit on the high-rise benches and feigning a little interest in the game. That way, I also picked up the lingo of pots, cannons and double cannons.

Secretly, I thought that since I was an ace shooter adept with guns and pistols, which these boys had never handled, I would probably not cut a sorry figure at the tables. But striking a billiard ball turned out to be far trickier. However, with practice and the encouragement of a few well-meaning players, I was soon able to strike the balls. When Mussoorie shut down for the winters, the billiard parlours remained the only place one could keep warm on winter evenings. The room would be filled with the bluish haze of cigarette smoke and resound to an occasional round of applause when one happened to play a particularly tricky shot.

Ballroom dancing was quite the craze during those years in Mussoorie. The two hotels, Savoy and Hakman's, offered good dancing floors, while the Royal Café cleared a small square patch for anyone who dared to dance on the handkerchief-sized dance floor. My father, preparing me for life in high society, enrolled me in the dancing classes run by one Mr. Benkovsky who would also perform the cabaret with his wife sometimes at Hakman's or the Savoy. While Mr. Benkovsky cranked up the gramophone and put on a 78 rpm record on the turntable, his assistant, an Anglo-Indian girl with red lips, red nails, heavily rouged cheeks and short skirts, would put me through my paces in ballroom dancing. The first time I had to take position with one hand around her back and the other clasped in hers, I trembled like a leaf and broke out into a heavy sweat.

"Why are you shivering, boy?" she asked, "Haven't you held a girl in your arms before?" Girl indeed! She must have been thirty plus! Well, I soon got over the shivers and was quickly matching steps with her as she took me through the fox trot, quickstep, the rumba and the samba. I was even wiggling my bony hips better than her. At last came the day when Mr. Benkovsky invited my father and mother to a performance by young Master Sharma and the over-gilded Miss Lilly. How both of us jived and rocked to Elvis Presley! When Lilly fell backwards in one manoeuvre, and I deftly caught her in my outstretched arms, my father clapped delightedly. Mr. Benkovsky proudly declared that I was now ready for the dance floors of the Hakman's and Savoy. Graduating from his school of ballroom dancing, I taught my three sisters, two cousins and even my mother how to dance – free of charge!

Bebeji scowled and fretted and fumed saying dancing was evil and that I would one day bring disgrace to the family's good name. I would retort by saying that if it was so wicked, then how did she explain Lord Krishna dancing and prancing with the *gopis*, as the village belles were called, in the Brindaban gardens of her beloved Mathura[4] and Gokul[5]?

---

4 Birthplace of Lord Krishna.
5 The village in which he was raised by his foster parents.

Chapter 18

The Virgin and The Bihari

She had been on the shelf for all of thirty-five years.

Plain as dough and flat as a pancake, Savitri, unlike the heroine of *Ramayan*, was no man's fantasy. Her face was pallid, and she wore her hair oiled and drawn back tight into a plait that resembled a long earthworm. Devoid of any trace of make-up, her pale face, with its rather large nose, did not usually invite a second glance. Her head was always covered by a chaste, white dupatta, and her mouth drawn into a perpetually sombre expression. Yet, like most Plain Janes, she would at times crack a smile that reached right up and into her eyes. They would, then, literally sparkle with life.

She was the apple of her mother's eye and the mote in her sister-in-law's. Both mother and daughter were crabbity creatures, whining constantly about this and that and always looking for the slightest excuse to clamp their claws around my mother's throat for imagined insults and minor slights. While her daughter could do no wrong, her daughter-in-law could do no right. Her worst sin, I think, in their eyes, was that she was fair and beautiful, whereas both of them were mirror images of each other. While our father obviously basked in the beauty of his wife, especially when it was the subject of praise from the high society of Mussoorie – he doted on his mother and sister and allowed himself to be craftily manipulated by them.

Since our family had been rather affluent in the pre-Partition era in Pakistan, Savitri had begun getting marriage proposals from a relatively young age. However, our grandmother found some reason or the other to nix the proposals. The real reason I suspect was that she was terrified of losing her staunch ally in the on-going battle with her daughter-in-law. Two against one was a more formidable rapid action force than one against one. I also think the daughter herself didn't want to be separated from her mother. So comfortable was she in the cocoon of her mother and brother's love that the very idea of having to marry and move into another family environment scared the living daylights out of her.

So it happened that when the family moved to Mussoorie, Savitri still remained unwed and unconcerned about her state. And so did her mother. Even in Mussoorie, whenever my father would put forward an eligible bachelor, he was promptly admonished and told to worry about his elder daughter instead who was by now studying in Junior Cambridge. Savitri, to remain in the good books of her brother, doted on his children. She helped us with our homework, got us dressed and fed and sent off to school in the mornings, and generally fussed around us.

As children, we naturally responded to such attention. Our mother, on the other hand, was elbow-deep in the kitchen, cooking for a family of eight plus five servants, not counting the innumerable guests that would land up during the summer and stay for months before they left for the plains. In between, she would have to cross swords or draw daggers with my grandmother and aunt (Savitri), collectively and individually. Naturally, she didn't have any time left to attend to, nor shower much affection on us. She would often bitterly remonstrate that we behaved as if Savitri was our mother and not her, and would unwittingly push us more toward our aunt. This suited Savitri's devious motives for her wicked aim was to alienate us from our mother and to isolate her further. On the other hand, our grandmother genuinely loved us although she didn't show it by her word or deed. But when she smiled at us, we knew deep inside that she loved us. She was not an attractive woman but when she smiled, her face took on a radiance that glowed like the sun as it appears from behind a dark cloud.

However, I am digressing. This story is about how Savitri, who unknown to anyone in the house, was secretly planning to shed her spinsterhood and the tag of a maiden 'left on the shelf'.

Since she was the only graduate of sorts in the family – she had done the Indian equivalent of B.A., and held a degree called *Vibhushan*-something from an odd place – she held her beaky, patrician nose rather high and kept looking down it most of the time. Her mornings were spent in devouring *The Times of India*, after my father was done with it. Her evenings were spent reading *Dharmayug*, a Hindi weekly that was popular in the early 1950s and '60s. A pair of reading glasses perched high on her nose, she would sit with her knees drawn up on the bed and spend a good hour or two reading the latest issue.

Dharmayug always featured two pieces of fiction in every issue. One would be a serialised novel and the other a short story. Savitri, who largely lived her life within its pages, followed the serials religiously. There was one author called Kamalnayan Chaudhary, whom she was particularly fond of. And unknown to anyone else in the family, she had secretly begun to correspond with him. The two-way traffic of 10 paise inland letters soon led to longer missives written on letter writing pads and stuffed thickly into the yellowish, pre-stamped envelopes embossed with the seal of the Ashoka Lion[1].

---

[1] The national emblem.

The postal exchanges between an upcoming author and our maiden un-fair soon blossomed into a Mills-and-Boon kind of romance. Savitri, emboldened by the long-distance attention she was getting, schemed to invite him to Delhi – all the way from Patna in Bihar.

The month was October. The year was 1956. Our father had just won the crossword of the *Illustrated Weekly of India* and there was great rejoicing, marred only by the fact that there were three other persons who had also won with all-correct entries and so the prize money was being divided among the four winners. Yet, it was a great achievement for my father who had been toiling at the crossword for years. To solve one clue, I remember taxying down with him, accompanied by another literati, to the Muslim University at Deoband in Uttar Pradesh. While I roamed around in the dusty cloisters of the place, he and his companion debated with the learned *moulvis*[2] over what could be the right answer to the tantalising clue. Satisfied that they had cracked the crossword, we returned that very evening to Mussoorie.

The celebrations culminated in a three-week holiday, away from the harsh winter of our hill station, for the whole family and Bahadru, one of our servants. Our first halt was Delhi at the same old Tees Hazari[3] Northern Railway Staff Quarters. Here, Savitri had schemed to meet her long distance, dhoti-kurta clad Bihari[4] lover. She had posted him the itinerary of our proposed journey, so he journeyed by train and came to tea one evening at Tees Hazari.

I do not remember much of that evening, being a callow youth of ten or twelve. All I recall is there were plenty of spicy snacks and sweetmeats to go around with tea. However,

---

2 Muslim scholar.
3 Named after a famous sessions court of old Delhi.
4 A native of the North-eastern state of Bihar.

I do remember that, in the end, she persuaded her brother to escort her to Darbhanga in Bihar the next summer. Our family pandit, who was instructed to bring his *panchang* – the booklet containing astrological charts and diagrams, also accompanied them. This was to be a recce of sorts into the family background of the Bihari suitor. That's how one fine morning, the three of them boarded the bus from Mussoorie to Delhi and from there caught the train that would take them to Darbhanga.

They returned ten days later. My father looked tired and unhappy. Savitri looked defiant, as if she had discovered she had a backbone after an excruciating long trip. My father spilled the unwelcome news. On making enquiries, the Bihari suitor turned out to be already-married. His wife, they said, lived in a remote village of Bihar, while the Casanova himself lived in a rented garret of sorts in Darbhanga. When accosted with the discovery, he vehemently denied his marriage and brazenly invited them to accompany him to his village in the back of beyond. The very thought of going deeper into dusty Bihar was repugnant to my father, as well as his sister. So they eventually decided to send panditji to the village to make further enquiries. Initially, my aunt pooh-poohed the town folks' talk as wicked gossip and insisted they were jealous of her suitor's success as a writer. She believed in her lover's integrity. My father had been left aghast at her defiant stand in the face of the evidence gathered. However, when the pandit returned to Mussoorie a week later with the damning bit of news, he mentioned that the Bihari also had two kids!

Savitri still insisted that the pandit was lying and wanted her to remain unwed. She even went so far as to hint that the pandit himself had his eyes on her! This confounded everyone. Her mother now called her a slut driven by lust for the Bihari Babu[5], and refused to talk to her. My mother, seizing the

---

[5] A native of Bihar.

opportunity she had been waiting for all these years, i.e., to get her sister-in-law off her back and drive a wedge between mother and daughter, sided with my aunt and persuaded, argued and prodded my father to go along and give his sister in marriage to the man, regardless of his marital status. The poor man, feeling helpless before the three women, succumbed to the suggestion.

The *mahurat*, the auspicious day for the marriage, got derived from the panchang. Three weeks from the set day of the marriage, I was asked to accompany my mother and aunt on their shopping spree for the wedding trousseau. My mother even parted with some of her gold (an action she would regret later), from which new ornaments could be made for my aunt. My father and grandmother were still dead set against the wedding but my mother, who was now in cahoots with my aunt, overrode their resistance.

The wedding was organised as a very private affair. There was no band-baaja. No one outside of the immediate family was present and the ceremonial rites were carried out one afternoon under the covered porch that extended from the main door of the house. The unblushing bride and the dark, dhoti-clad groom were then waved off to their honeymoon, of all places, to the holy city of Haridwar. An unholy marriage was going to be consummated in one of the holiest cities!

What happened in Haridwar is something I was unable to find out over the years. Since I can bet my aunt hadn't a clue about the sexual side of marriage, had she been revolted when the Bihari tried to disrobe and mount her? Did he try marital rape, or did he find her totally sexless (she was flat-chested if you recall and also had a faint moustache over her upper lip) and was repulsed? If my mother knew, she didn't breathe a word to us. The couple returned after four days to Mussoorie, and my aunt vowed that she would not go with her husband to his home in faraway Bihar. She dug her heels in. My mother was almost paralysed with shock at this unexpected turn of events. Gloom and doom descended upon the house.

Years passed. My aunt never budged from the house. The Bihari Babu was forbidden entry in Mussoorie. The bickering became bitterer. Mother and daughter united to hassle my mother, their common foe, once again. A decade later, the phone rang one fine day. The caller said the Bihari Babu had died after a short illness in hospital. The aunt beat her chest and wailed for five minutes. I clapped my hands to my ears to shut out the wailing. My mother smirked with an expression that at last Savitri had got her just desserts. My father couldn't have cared less.

And life went on as usual.

Chapter 19

A Trigger-happy Colonel

'Jeremy... *Je-rrr-e-mmyy!*' The walrus-moustachioed Colonel Roberts would start bellowing every morning around seven to wake up his fat little son for school, failing which he would occasionally fire a shot in the air. The Colonel's booming voice and the gunshot would echo in Happy Valley, but its first full blast would roll down our red tin roof, as our house was just below his, and shatter the morning stillness of the hills.

While my sisters and I would trudge up the steep path, carrying our schoolbags, that led from our house to the road above that led to the school, Jeremy would make his appearance astride a horse, Sola hat held firmly by a leather strap under his wobbly chin, munching on a thick sandwich. "Good mo-rrrr-ning," Jeremy would sing-song in his reed-thin voice as he waved and rode past. Jeremy hated going to school on horseback. He disliked the flea-ridden horse, the grimy saddle and the unwashed horse owner who kept flicking a stick on the horse's hind to keep it going. The day the horse wouldn't turn up, little Jeremy would wait for us outside the creaky green gate of Tullahmore Lodge, the sprawling, somewhat dilapidated bungalow that was at a rise above our house. Piglet-pink Jeremy would huff and puff with the weight of his schoolbag as he tried to keep pace with us as we hurried to our school.

You may well wonder where Jeremy's mother was while all this commotion went on every morning at Tullahmore Lodge? A mousy, frail-looking woman, she probably stayed put in her bed and did not rise till noon. It seemed she was a woman of no consequence in the house of Colonel Roberts. When the gun-toting Colonel was away on one of his hunts in the jungles, one would occasionally catch sight of her draped languidly over the wooden rails of the curved balcony that ran right around the front of their house. Sometimes, while returning from school, we would spot her standing by the green gate waiting for Jeremy to come around the bend in the road. She would then smile weakly and flutter her hand in a wave as we passed by.

One Sunday morning, we saw a ragged band of villagers led by the milkman, who delivered cans of milk to our house every morning, walking down the slope towards our house. They asked one of the servants to tell 'Panditji', as my dad was deferentially addressed, that they had come to meet him on an urgent business. As my dad stepped out to meet them, they started at once:

"*Panditji, Panditji... hum to sab barbaad ho gaye!*"[1]

"*Kal raat, baagh mera bachda uttha kar le gaya!*"[2]

"*Panditji, hamari toh jaan par ban aayi hai! Aap chalo apni bandook le kar hamare saath!*"[3]

By this time, my grandmother, my aunt, and my mother had also gathered around and started warning my father, "*Kahin nahi jaana, kahin nahi jaana!*"[4]

"*Arrey Memsahib,*" the villagers wailed, "*Hamare baal bachhon,*

---

[1] Panditji, Panditji... we are all ruined!
[2] Last night, the leopard took my calf away!
[3] Panditji, our lives are at stake! Get your gun and please come with us!
[4] You are not going anywhere.

gaaye bakriyon ka kya hoga? Baagh toh unhe khaa jaayega!"[5]

Pacifying the villagers on one hand and the womenfolk on the other, my dad told them, "*Ruko, ruko... chalo hum sab shikari Colonel ko ja kar milte hain... woh jaroor sab ki maddad karenge,*"[6] and led them, with me tagging along, up the Colonel's lodge.

The Colonel who had been watching the commotion from his balcony, seeing my father and the villagers approach, came down carrying his gun. Come to think of it, I rarely saw him without the gun... and often wondered whether he even slept with it by his side – or perhaps between him and his wife!

"What's all the hullabaloo about, Mr. Sharma?" And without pausing for an answer, turned to the villagers asking, "*Yeh kya sab tum halla-gulla machaa rakha hai?*" "*Tum sab danda kyun le kar aaye hai?*"[7] My father explained that a leopard had been terrorising the village folk for the past month or so and they, having heard that a fearless and ferocious hunter was living among us, had come to seek his help in ridding the village of this animal that was preying on their goats and cattle.

"*Hunter saab*[8], *aaj hamari gaaye bakri ko maar raha hai, kal hamare bachhey ko uthaa le jaayega toh hum kya karenge, sahib!*"[9] chorused the villagers. At this point, the headman stepped forward with folded hands, and begged the Colonel to come to their rescue. The Colonel turned to my father and said, "Mr. Sharma, we must do something forthwith. You pick your

---

5 Oh Memsahib, what will happen to our children and our cows and goats. The leopard will take them away.

6 Wait, wait... all of us will go and meet the hunter Colonel... he will help you all.

7 What's all the noise and commotion about? Why are you all carrying such big sticks?

8 A polite addressing reserved for a gentleman

9 Hunter sahib, today he is killing our cows and goats, tomorrow if he takes our children what will we do?

guns and let's plan the hunt!" My father, who had never handled a gun in his life although he had guns of every kind in the house, visibly paled under his dark skin and giving a sheepish grin said, "Colonel Sahib, you are the hunter of tigers and lions, not I!" To soften the blow, he said, "But you can take whichever guns you want from me and the cartridges as well."

The Colonel harrumphed, snorted, and shrugged, "Oh, very well, we could use an extra gun or two..! But I think you should accompany us on the big hunt. And I won't hear another word on it!" He said this by thumping the barrel of his gun on the floor. There and then, they drew a plan that the Colonel and my dad would go that weekend for a recce of the village, and chart out the site of the hunt with the help of the villagers.

It was decided that a goat would be tied to a tree on the outskirts of the village as bait for the leopard or tiger – the accounts of the villagers were so confusing, the Colonel couldn't quite determine which animal he was going to hunt. Along with my father, he instructed the villagers on the exact height, width, location and the distance of the *machaan*, or shooting tower with a platform, from the tree that the goat would be tethered to for the big hunt. The village drummers were told to draw their drums tight and taut so when beaten upon with drumsticks, they would, if required, create such a din and clamour that would confuse and drive the big cat in the direction they wanted.

On the day of the hunt, my grandmother and aunt made such a hue and cry about my father accompanying the Colonel on the hunt that he shamefacedly had to back out and send two of his servants along instead. My mother sneered at this obvious display of cowardice and backing down by my father. But the wails and breast-beating by our grandmother and aunt would have driven any man into submission. Around four in the afternoon, with the Colonel leading the hunting party of servants who had never fired a gun in their lives, they left for

Kandigaon – the village that was being terrorised by the wild creature. The Colonel, besides commandeering my father's guns, also made off with a box of cartridges and his powerful set of Zeiss binoculars.

They were gone for two days and returned dejected, empty-handed on the third. The leopard or tiger, whatever it was, had decided not to show up for the hunter on the first night. On the second night, it had foraged in another nearby village for its prey. Two days later, the villagers were back – this time with longer faces that fell right down to their knees. Leading them was a tearful woman whose husband had been mauled and killed by the wild cat, the night before. He had apparently stepped out of his hut to answer the call of nature, and not returned. The woman, seeing the hut empty the next morning, raised a hue and cry and the villagers, armed with *lathis*[10], went looking for him in the jungles. All they found was a trail of blood, his muddied white dhoti and an empty *lota* (vessel) by the bushes.

"*Bahut hua!* Enough, enough!" barked the Colonel, "*Rona-dhona band karo! Iss baar mein uss kambakht baagh ko kachha chabba jaaoonga,*" meaning that this time he would chew on the raw meat of that wretched animal. The villagers, upon hearing this dreaded threat, cheered loudly and the Colonel's chest swelled in his khaki bush shirt. This time, he announced, another hunter friend called Tommy would also be joining the hunt, and he instructed the villagers to tie a nice, meaty goat to the tree.

I whined and pleaded with my parents to let me go, but my pleas fell on deaf ears.

The hunting party left for Kandigaon on a Friday afternoon. Two of our servants, who formed the hunting party, later told us that the Colonel even went to the extent of offering flowers and sweets to the village deity to enlist his aid in the big kill.

---

10 Batons.

Soon after sunset, they began swigging the Hercules XXX army rum from their hip flasks while the villagers killed and roasted a plump rooster for them. Warmed by the rum and fed on the rooster, they pulled out their cheroots and began discussing the likelihood of the wild cat turning up tonight, with the village headman and the others who were gathered around a bonfire. Suddenly, one of the villagers whispered "Sshhh... *Chupp!*" and pointed his finger towards the tethered goat that, with its head cocked at an angle, had started quivering uncontrollably. A deathly silence fell over the assembled party. The Colonel stealthily crept up to the machaan on the tree; Tommy, who had earlier selected another vantage point for himself, climbed up another tree. Everyone moved quickly but noiselessly to their appointed places.

The other servant now took up the narrative: "*Mein-nnn, mein-nn-nn,*" the goat began to bleat in a high-pitched sound. It had started shivering badly now, and this time it also emptied its bowels. The Colonel silently cocked his rifle, as did Tommy on his perch. The cheroots were snuffed out and the tension in the air was electric. There was a soft rustling in the bushes as the animal prowled stealthily, sniffing out the ground. A pair of glowering eyes appeared and disappeared in the bushes as it moved. The Colonel squeezed his eyes to keep his focus sharp on its movements and made a hand signal to Tommy, who was also alert to the presence of the animal within their midst. Tommy waved a white cloth in the direction of the others on the ground.

The silence of the night was rent by the deafening clamour of drumbeats. All of a sudden, the wild animal leapt from the bushes. As it did, the Colonel pressed the trigger and the bullet whizzed through the air. Another bullet from Tommy thudded into the animal while it was still in mid-air before it collapsed and landed just inches besides the goat that set up another round of bleating. Cries, cheers, drumbeats tore through the night as the entire village now rushed out. The Colonel and Tommy were lifted high on the young men's shoulders and paraded in a circle around the dead animal. Peace and safety had returned to the village at last.

The next morning, the hunting party arrived home carrying the dead tiger hanging upside down with its four legs tied to a long pole, which was being carried by four people at the front, and four at the back of the pole. The Colonel fired two shots in the air to announce his triumphal return, and we rushed up the slope to Tullahmore Lodge. There lay the dead beast. The Colonel was kneeling by its side with a yellow tape measure in his hands. "Ten feet in length – from nose to tail!" he announced with pride. Everyone clapped and cheered. Fat little Jeremy was tugging at the tiger's tail. I personally received a 'claw' from the tiger's paw as a memento from the Colonel, which I have with me to this day.

Colonel Roberts' exploit was the talk of the town for months! His photograph that showed him standing with one foot on the tiger's neck, with the butt of his gun resting on the beast's haunches, and one hand twirling his moustache, appeared in *The Mussoorie Times* and the local paper of Dehradun. My father, on cue, decided on the spot that he would make a hunter of me. He bought me first an air gun with a packet of pellets and a target board, and saw to it that I practiced every day until one day I hit the bull's eye. I was then encouraged to go on small hunting trips to perfect my aim, accompanied by my young servant boy. One day, I shot him on his round buttock with one of the rubber pellets, and my air gun was confiscated for a week. After a year or so, my father presented me with a .22 air rifle with which I became the bane of *langoors* – the white-haired, black-faced baboons of the Himalayas.

Chapter 20

The Farmer of Happy Valley

Now that I was ready to become a young hunter, my father pulled out his Smith & Wembley single barrel gun and cartridges and took me along to meet young John Taylor, the Anglo-Indian gent who ran the local dairy in Happy Valley and who was also a hunter of sorts. This was testified by the occasional brace of wild pheasants he would send to my father, as gratitude I supposed, for the vast amounts of milk which the family and its retainers consumed during the course of one day!

As we entered the gates, one of which bore the legend 'Taylor Cottage' engraved in a brass plaque, while the arch above the gate was emblazoned with the words 'Taylor Milk Dairy', I saw a long, rather narrow cottage that looked like a large train coach running alongside the path. Its frontage was made up of several square glass panes set in green, wooden framework along which climbed vines blooming with primroses. We rang the doorbell and the voice of an old man called out, "Come in, come in, the door is open." I was introduced as "This is my Prince of Wales" (a reference I abhorred, as Prince Charles, the current prince of Wales was not only chubby but also jug-eared) to the older Mr. Taylor who, attired in a navy blue suit and tie, was comfortably ensconced in a rather large armchair and was puffing blue smoke from his cigar. "Sit down; sit down, Mr. Sharma... John will be here any minute, he's out feeding the cows," he said.

John breezed in flashing a bright smile and running his fingers through his light brown hair that was parted on the side. Blue-eyed, fair and ruddy-cheeked, John was dressed as usual in a rough tweed jacket and rumpled trousers that were bagging at the knees – from too much kneeling besides the cows, I thought. He paused to give me a quick handshake and said, "Be right back with you Sharmaji," at my father before dashing into one of the rooms of the cottage. "I don't know what to do about this boy... he works himself to the bone, getting up at four in the morning," grumbled the older Taylor, rather fondly.

Soon, John came out rubbing his hands and pulling up a chair sat beside his dad on the verandah. Tommy, his pet cocker spaniel, waddled in to sit by his feet and John ruffled the hair below the dog's neck. "John," said the elder Taylor, "Mr. Sharma here would like you to teach his son how to shoot a gun." John grinned and said, "Of course, of course..." and giving me a solid thump on the back, added, "We will soon make a fine marksman out of him."

That's when it was decided that every Saturday afternoon I would appear at the Taylor Dairy with my servant who would be toting the gun. John would then take us deeper into the valley, where we could do target practice. He would instruct me on how to shoot at the trunk of this tree, or the branch of that tree, increasing the distance of the target each time. As the gun fired, it would jolt my shoulder and the bullet would go anywhere but where it was meant to go. However, after a couple of weeks, I learnt to control the jolt, hold the gun steady, aim sharp, and shoot straight.

The double-barrelled gun was harder to manage with its double-triggers that were highly sensitive to the touch.

One had to be absolutely sure that if one was aiming to fire the left barrel, then one had to press the trigger that was in front and not, accidentally, the second trigger that lay close behind the first. Learning to fire both the barrels in quick succession was even harder. The wisps of blue smoke that curled from the barrels would assault my nostrils with an acrid smell. Just firing the guns was not enough. After the target practice got over, John would take me back to the cottage where he would teach me how to dismantle, clean, grease and reassemble the guns.

John was a kind, young man and a very patient one at that. He was also handsome-looking. Come to think of it, it's surprising that none of the local, convent-educated girls went after him, for to me, he appeared a highly eligible bachelor. However, I recall that a distant cousin from his mother's side had been living with them for some years now in the cottage. She was a rather stocky girl called Sally, who braided her hair into two plaits and then tied them overlapping each other on top of her head. I also remember that she was always wearing an apron and used to keep wiping her hands on it. She was a big help to John's mother in looking after the production side of the dairy, and the old lady was rather keen to make a match of her with John. He, of course, didn't seem to be making any move in that direction. The old lady passed away without seeing her cherished wish fulfilled.

John was a loner. In fact, the whole family usually kept to themselves. The women rarely stepped out of their cottage and, of course, old Mr. Taylor didn't either except, perhaps, for that one visit when he had come to tea at our house. For some odd reason, my father got along rather well with him and he would drop in now and then at their cottage in Happy Valley. When the old lady passed on, the elder Mr. Taylor sent for my father one day and apparently asked him to intercede on his behalf with John in the matter of Sally. I really don't know how successful my father was but sometime later, their wedding took place.

My parents and I had gone over one evening to offer congratulations with a wedding present and Sally, who was now pushing thirty-six or so (she was about five years older to John), looked quite the beaming bride with a broad toothy smile that never seemed to leave her face. She kept fussing over John who seemed rather embarrassed by her attentions and kept blushing most of the evening. Wafer-thin cucumber sandwiches, hot scones and cake topped with fresh dairy cream were served accompanied by an aromatic pot of tea.

One night, old Mr. Taylor breathed his last. My father and I went to the cottage the next morning to pay our respects. He seemed at peace as he lay, wearing his blue suit, with his pipe stuffed into the upper pocket of his jacket, and his white hair spread like a halo around his cherubic face in the coffin. I thought to myself that the reason he looked so peaceful lying there was the fact that he had finally done his duty by getting John hitched to Sally, and could now convey the good news to his wife when he came across her in Heaven. I don't quite remember if he was buried in the grounds of the dairy or at the cemetery over on Camel Back Road.

Alas, the old order changeth yielding place to the new and Taylor Cottage was no longer the quiet, peaceful, laid-back dairy that ran on its own steam. A new broom sweeps clean, they say. And when a white witch is riding the broom, it sweeps absolutely clean. Yes, John was nothing short of bewitched as Sally more or less relegated him to old Mr. Taylor's armchair and she now, quite literally, wore the pants in the house. New hands were hired at the dairy and under the efficient management of Sally, the dairy prospered. Besides the staple milk, it now also offered its customers fresh cream and butter, bread and biscuits baked by the new Mrs. Taylor. Soon, it also got a fresh, green coat of paint and the old, fading and worn out chintz curtains were replaced with crisp new ones. The dairy changed more ways than one, but what remained the same was the two plaited braids piled atop Sally's head.

Sad to say, the Taylors, unlike their hens and roosters, never produced any offspring. John's brown hair became flecked with grey. His skin lost its ruddiness for lack of sunshine, as he now took to staying indoors. Sally's complexion, paradoxically, now radiated dewdrop freshness. While he grew thinner, Sally became stouter.

Later, when I came home during the semester break from my college in Delhi, I heard they had adopted a *pahari* (hill) girl, who was the daughter of one of their workers at the dairy. A few years down the line, they adopted her younger sister as well. When the Tibetans came and settled in Happy Valley, John got some kind of reprieve. I heard he had been hired to teach English to the young Tibetan children.

Chapter 21

Guns and Roses

It was a cold, starless night. From the glass-paned windows that ran along the side of the room that overlooked the valley below, the hills appeared to shift and undulate as the wind bent the branches and whistled through the leaves of the pine and oak trees. Swaddled in layers of warm clothes and mufflers, we were sitting around the metal stove in which the coals and logs of wood crackled and burnt, cupping mugs filled with hot milk. My sister was telling us a ghost story when, suddenly, our dog Bingo cocked his ears hearing, before we could, a faint drone and then the deafening roar that reverberated in the skies.

Our aunt came running out of her room clutching her shawl. "*Hai Rabba, au ki si?*"[1] she said in a trembling voice. "Probably a jet that just broke through the sound barrier," I said. "No," insisted my sister, "It sounded like an explosion." The telephone rang shrilly, it was our dear neighbour Mrs. Gantzer, sounding petrified, "Gattu, did you all hear that explosion? I think a bomb has fallen on Gun Hill!"

I was astounded, "A bomb? Why should bombs be falling here!?" I asked. "Didn't you hear the news?" she said, "India

---

[1] "Oh God, what was that?"

and Pakistan have declared war on one another!" "What!!" I exclaimed. "Yes, and I just received a call from the District Magistrate, Mr. Raturi," she said. "Please put out all your lights, right away! He has ordered a complete blackout. Don't even burn a candle," she added.

There were no newspapers the next day or, rather, there was no delivery by the newspaper boy, but the radio proclaimed war, all day. From then on, the air was rend with screaming jets and soon we got accustomed to them shooting across the blue Himalayan skies leaving parallel trails of white clouds as they sped towards the borders. It was a time of tension and rumours flew thick and fast...

...The enemy had landed by parachutes on Lal Tibba, the highest point in Mussoorie.

...Two Pakistani infiltrators wearing *burqas*[2] had been caught, stripped and handed over at the police *chowky*[3].

...A cache of hand grenades had been recovered from the Municipal school.

...A bomb had exploded near the clock tower in Landour.

...The army would soon be patrolling the Mall in Mussoorie.

Our grandmother quite irrationally said it was the fault of my mother for putting the family's lives in danger. If my mother hadn't goaded my father to flee Pakistan after Partition, we would still be sitting comfortably in the security of our homes there! Besides which, she welcomed the war, saying that soon Mussoorie would be occupied by Pakistan and we would then be easily able to return to our ancestral home in Sialkot. How could one deal with such convoluted logic of the old woman?

Not a single rumour was substantiated. All proved to be

---

[2] A black, body-covering garment that Muslim women wear when they step out of the house.

[3] Outpost.

false alarms, some pranks played by the local loafers. Other weird rumours being floated around were the products of fevered minds. The war never came anywhere close near Mussoorie, and nor to the Doon valley. Anyhow, the next day the kids were rushed off to the local bookstore to buy reams of black poster paper which had to be taped on all the windows, and there were dozens of them, to the house. This house, Shamrock Lodge, seemed to be made out of windows and should have been rightly named 'Whispering Windows' or 'Rattling Windows'.

However, for the days the window dressing drive lasted; it proved to be rather exciting. Later, we would go for our evening strolls on the Mall clutching pen torches and covering their narrow beams of light with our gloved fingers. Since all street lights were kept switched off, some of us would troop up to the Imperial Billiards Room and pass our evenings playing snooker and billiards in a hall whose large windows had been draped with yards of black cloth. Most of us sported dark-coloured clothes so that Pakistani soldiers, who could be lying in ambush around the next corner, wouldn't be able to spot us easily.

The fallout of the war in Mussoorie turned out to be much ado about nothing. But we went on to make a song and dance of it, albeit with a patriotic hue. This was still mid-October; the schools were wrapping up their annual exams. The students would leave for their respective homes for the winter vacations by the first week of December. We had to get our act together fast, and we did. My two sisters, their friends, my friends and I got together one evening at our house to discuss how we could do our bit for the armed forces currently engaged in fighting a winter war with the enemy on our borders. Short of joining the armed forces, which we were too young to do anyway, unlike the Mujahideen who recruit boys as young as ten-years-old, we explored other ways of raising money for the War Fund.

Remember, this was 1964. It was most definitely not the year of rock shows, jazz yatras, and such events. Forget that, even television hadn't made its appearance! So we thought of putting up a 'Variety Show' of song, dance and drama – to appeal to a cross section of the Mussoorie residents. We were an eclectic group – Rana, a gardener's son; Surbir, an electric meter reader's son; Raj and Rajiv, a millionaire's son and daughter; Uday, an usher at the local cinema hall; Gurinder, a doctor's daughter; Geeta, the college Principal's daughter; Suresh, the telephone operator's son; Jhabru, a strikingly handsome Nepalese gadabout, and others. Hindus, Christians, Muslims, Sikhs, Buddhists – all came together. Above all, there was Ruskin Bond, the well-known author of children's books.

One day, all of us barged into the Hakman's Hotel and *gheraoed*[4] the proprietor to request that he contribute his mite to the war effort by allowing us to stage our Variety Show for two days in the grand ballroom of his hotel that was equipped with a superb stage and lights – free of charge. With some pressure brought to bear upon him by the millionaire's offspring and one of the actors whose father was police superintendent – the manager acquiesced gracefully to our request.

Rehearsals began in full swing at Hakman's Hotel, that was completely overtaken by the dancing troupe. As winter had already set in, there were hardly any guests besides an odd honeymooning couple. Convincing the parents of a few girls to let their daughters dance and prance on stage was quite a task. In one case, we even had to convince the elder sister of one of the girls (who herself had been educated in London in the early 1950s and was separated from her husband, in the days when such things were unheard of in Indian society) to let her younger sibling dance on stage with a chowkidar's son! An appeal to their patriotic quotient was the last nail in the

---

[4] Surrounded.

coffin of their resistance. They had no argument when confronted with this ploy and finally gave their reluctant consent. Two stuck-up sisters of a hotelier, who had initially refused to join the show, on second thought asked to be given some role in the show, but everyone vetoed their inclusion. For a while, they were pariah.

Once the cast and crew of actors, dancers, musicians, light boys, stagehands, and prompters had assembled, the show was on the road. Posters for the show went up in shops, schools and restaurants of the hill resort. The appeal, somewhat plagiarised and adapted from the famous phrase 'Ask not what the country can do for you, but what you can do for the country,' pleaded that the least the students and residents could do was fork out Rs. 50 or Rs. 20 for the War Fund in the form of tickets for the show. Sure enough, the tickets began to sell off pretty fast from the bookshops, cinema counters, and the restaurants at which they had been made available.

Volunteers went to all the schools clutching wads of tickets to sell to the teachers and students. Not surprisingly, it was the boys' schools that bought most tickets, seeing in it an opportunity to ogle and whistle at the local girls, as they pranced around on the stage.

The master of ceremonies finished his ranting about the enemy on our borders and the courage of our soldiers who were protecting them, so we could enjoy an evening of entertainment. He then declared grandiosely, "On with the Show!" (the signal for the curtains to part at the centre like the Red Sea), but the pulleys to draw the curtains apart snagged. Two boys immediately ran up and manually pulled the curtains, revealing two dancers caught off-guard. While the music had begun, the dancers were out of step. The audience tittered and booed. Suddenly, the music stopped, the dancers froze in their poses, and came to life again once it restarted. Jerkily, the show went on.

The Hill Billy

Indian theatre has a long tradition of men impersonating female characters and playing them to androgynous perfection. Our show did a role reversal on this time-honoured tradition. My sister, older to me by a couple of years, was chosen to enact the role of the Buddha[5], mainly because she was the tallest girl in the group and didn't have to utter a word, leave alone sing, throughout a three-act silent play that had singers offstage narrating his life in a kind of semi-opera. At that distance, no one guessed it was a girl playing the Buddha, so it went off without a hitch or a snitch.

Ruskin Bond, whose name pulled its weight to swell the audience, had been persuaded to direct a one-act English comedy called 'A Rose for Miss Fisher'. A scene required me to pour tea and hand over the cup to Miss Fisher who was played by a simpering shop girl. Instructions had been issued that the pot should contain piping hot tea, because when Miss Fisher was to take the first sip, she was to scald her lips so I could put the balm of my twenty-one year old lips on hers. The tea tray was brought in by the maid and set on the table. When I moved to make the cup of tea, nothing poured out of the teapot... it was empty! And I had already, simultaneous with the action of pouring the tea, started to mouth my dialogue: "This is the finest, most fragrant Darjeeling tea you will ever taste." I bent the teapot some more, thinking perhaps someone backstage had filled only a half or quarter of it, and the lid fell down with a clatter on the wooden boards and wouldn't stop rolling across the stage. To our horror, it rolled down the wooden steps and came to a stop at the foot of one of the privileged guests sitting in the first row on a sofa.

I forgot the rest of my dialogue; the prompter's whisper was two lines ahead of me. Miss Fisher looked frantically left, then right and then straight at the audience. In the confusion,

---

5 Gautam Buddha, the founder of Buddhism.

I lost the chance of kissing the belle of Mussoorie. The curtain was hastily drawn, and even more hastily pulled back in the commotion to reveal all of us cursing each other on stage. This proved to be even more hilarious for the audience, as they hooted with laughter and the boys from the boys' schools catcalled and whistled. Well, you would have thought that was the end of the play, but it wasn't. The cast gamely apologised for the interruption and proceeded to play the rest of it out, and the sympathetic audience gave us a smattering of applause – for the comedy within the comedy, I guess.

The show netted a tidy sum. It wasn't the super-duper hit that we expected it to be, but it did serve to bring the who's who of Mussoorie to rub shoulders and mingle with the shopkeepers and municipal clerks and peons in a show of patriotism. Of course, this camaraderie wouldn't last. Pretty soon, everyone went back into their respective social closets. But, for those two days, we had achieved the impossible. The money collected was handed over to the District Magistrate of Dehradun, who allowed us to deduct a little, over and above the expenses incurred. This was enough for an outdoor picnic, organised a month later for the entire cast and crew of plumbers' sons, electricians' nephews, shopkeepers' daughters and the first citizenrys' brats.

After a fortnight or so, the blackout of Mussoorie that had been observed more in its violation than observation, was officially lifted and the hills twinkled again with lights flickering from its mansions, cottages and street lamps.

Chapter 22

Our Lady of the 'Clucks'

Her eyebrows were finely pencilled arches. Her lipsticked mouth looked like a luscious red cherry. Her hair in the fashion of those days was styled in tight curls. And she wore pants when the rest of the Anglo-Indian ladies wore pale, pastel dresses with floppy hats and walked around with lace-edged handkerchiefs held daintily to their nose. She was a lady who was at once revered, feared and dreaded as much by the hoi polloi as she was by the officialdom and serfdom. Her voice could be heard booming from a mile off as she walked up the steep climb to the Mall Road, which she would often negotiate twice a day from her cottage that lay in a deep cleft below the Library Bazaar.

Evening walks are almost a religion with the permanent residents of a hill station in India. Everyone, including the owners of shops, step out on the Mall for the evening parade of glamour and the ritual of salaams, namastes, howdy do's and gossip. The sweepers on the road would stand aside with their heads bowed and brooms held behind their backs when they got a whiff of Mrs. Ingram's perfume, which travelled a good distance ahead of her. As she passed, they would bow low, raise their hand to their foreheads and murmur '*Salaam Memsaab*' which she acknowledged with a barely noticeable nod of her head.

The *ghodawallas*, as she called the boys who ran behind the ponies on the *kuccha*[1] path along the side of the metallled road, with tourists in the saddle, would immediately rein in the ponies and madly flap their hands, usually in vain, to make the dust settle if they spotted her coming. I've heard them say that at times even their ponies shat with fright if they smelt her coming! She would cover her nose, glare at them and the riders, muttering, "Mussoorie is going to the dogs!" as she passed by.

Occasionally, on spotting our family on the Mall, she would stop to greet my parents. She gave me quite a scare one day when pointing one of her long, red nails at me and prodding my frail chest with it, she admonished my father, "Oh, *toh yeh tumhara Prince of Wales hai... gosh, kitna patla dubla hai, Mr. Sharma!*"[2] Then turning to me she added, "Are you still going to that girls' school up the road? You should be in St. Georges by now young fella, just like my Tommy." Then glancing up and down at my mother, she would condescendingly include her in the exchange by remarking, "*Oh Mrs. Sharma, sari kitna achha pehna hai aaj.*"[3]

She was the one to pass along this gem of slanderous gossip about the bungalow we lived in. Apparently, the Nawab had built this lovely, double-storey bungalow in the thick of the forest for his third Begum who was still in her early-twenties while he was on the wrong side of fifty. "And, now Mr. Sharma, you have brought your Begum to live here!" she would add and cackle raucously at her own wit. Of course, there was no such yawning age difference between my parents, but Betty, which was her Christian name, had to have her little joke at someone's expense.

---

1 Unpaved, dust ridden path.

2 Oh, so this is your Prince of Wales... gosh, what a thin-stick he is!

3 Oh Mrs. Sharma, what a nice sari you are wearing.

She meant no harm; she just loved to add the spice of malice to her sharp tongue that was always clucking at something or the other. Whenever she spied my spinster aunt, she would get on her case saying, "Savitri, why isn't your brother finding a good husband for you... so many eligible men in the town... but my dear, you shouldn't dress so dowdily... look at you, all covered from head to toe like some baniya shopkeeper's daughter! And, no makeup! No wonder you look so anaemic!"

As children, we didn't know her beyond those infrequent run-ins on the Mall and usually, when seeing her coming from afar, we would scuttle away and hide inside a shop. Once, she caught me as I was slipping into one of the shops below the Mussoorie Public Library that occupied the floor above. She was just turning towards the stairway that led up to the Library, but had stopped in her tracks after spying me. Her arm shot out... her hand grabbed me by the scruff of my neck and she gave me a good rattle.

"Prince of Wales, indeed!" she scoffed, "Don't they teach you any manners at that girls' school you go to? Just you wait till I tell that Miss Jansen of yours! Hasn't she taught you to wish your elders when you see them?" I half-stuttered, half-choked out "Errr-rr...errr-rrr... good morning Mrs. Ingram, I-I-I-I didn't see you coming... really," and tried to prise loose from her vice-like grip. "Hmm... a liar too... you badmaash," she said as her eyebrows arched and almost disappeared into the curls banging on her forehead. "I have a good mind to make you dust all the books in my Library, but this time I will let you go... so run along!" And run I did as she let go of my collar and gave me a push to propel me off the verandah.

The years rolled by...

In 1963, victims of adversity, we moved residence from Happy Valley to a small cottage that stood midway between the Library Bazaar and Kincraig, one of the entry points to Mussoorie.

The cottage, Shamrock Lodge, was shaped rather queerly like a railway coach in the sense that it was longitudinally designed with four rooms that ran in two parallel lengths, much like train tracks, and three toilets just as oddly placed – one, almost at the entrance to the cottage, the second in between two rooms and, a third at the extreme end of the cottage. The kitchen, as was the style then, was apart from the house. It was on a rise and had to be accessed by climbing four high steps to its door. In front of the cottage was a gravelled compound with a rather stunted, sorry-looking and solitary apricot tree that flowered beautifully in spring but bore sour fruit fit only for the crows.

However, the unique feature of this cottage was that it stood right above the rather stately mansion of Mrs. Ingram's residence called, I think rather appropriately, 'Laughing Brook'. To my mind, 'Cackling Brook' would have suited it better, because Mrs. Ingram didn't laugh... she always cackled! We were dumbstruck when we realised who our distinguished neighbour was going to be... the Iron Lady herself!

Behind her house, she had built a large hen house populated by two roosters and a brood of hens. The front compound of the house had an ornamental stone bird-bath at its centre, and a kidney-shaped pond – almost a staple feature in most of the houses of Mussoorie – in which goldfish languidly swam or seemingly stood still with their unblinking eyes and gaping mouths. A garden umbrella with a white-painted, cast-iron bench and table stood in one corner. Along one side of the corridor, that one had to walk down before entering the living room, ran a wire netting behind which multi-coloured budgerigars tweeted and chirruped as they swung on their small bird-swings or just flew around the foliage inside the cage that wasn't really a cage.

Betty lived here with her retired husband, who had once

been a judge in a dusty district of Bihar. During the day, the judge always wore a dark suit with a tie, even if he was not stepping out of the house. Betty would sport colourful frocks with large floral prints. She would usually step out of her house wearing a hat, along with the judge, at around eleven in the morning, and together they would have their morning coffee seated under the garden umbrella that served as a sun-block for her porcelain complexion. While she brought him upto date on the latest gossip, he would puff at his cigar and nod absent-mindedly every now and then, to show he was listening.

Betty was on the invitee list of almost every official event that happened in our small hill resort. If she hadn't been, she would have blasted the 'good-for-nothing government clerk' responsible for the oversight, over the phone, and threatened to have him transferred to some godforsaken place. They quivered, quavered and always acquiesced. Even the high society of Mussoorie would not dare to strike her from their invitee list, although she turned down most of their invitations with an audible sniff of her nose and an angry puff on her cigarette. Since those were the days of straight, honest-to-goodness cigarettes, and not of the new-fangled, filter-tipped kinds, hats off to her for never ever using a dainty cigarette holder like the rest of the high society hens.

Betty's hens were the bane of my existence.

The roosters would start crowing at an unearthly hour, I think it would be around four or five in the morning, and my sleep would be shattered. Then would follow a non-stop exchange between the hens and the roosters. I would rush outside, grab a handful of gravel and throw it on the tin roof of the coop. That would quiet them down for a while. If I was feeling particularly vicious, I would throw another handful of gravel on Betty's roof as well, targeting her bedroom. One day, she trudged up the shortcut to our house and told my mother,

"Mrs. Sharma, aaj kal koi mere chhat par pathar marta hai subha subha... Mera neend bekar ho jata hai."[4]

My mother, although she knew it was me doing the dirty trick, feigned ignorance but added, *"Mrs. Ingram, aap ka murgi bhi bahut shor karta hai subaah-subaah."*[5] Betty cackled at that and said, *"But Mrs. Sharma, woh toh stupid janwar log hai, woh kya kar sakta hai!"*[6] My mother later told me that Mrs. Ingram had confided to her that she had secretly seen me one morning hurling the stones on her tin roof, but had told her not to say anything to me about it. I felt so guilty that for months after that, I avoided coming face to face with Betty.

The day one of the hens was decapitated for the couple's lunch or dinner, the hen house would be strangely quiet. I suppose they were pondering whose head would be next on Betty's chopping block! But it was rarely the hen she had pointed out to the *jamadaar*, her sweeper. Half-blind, he would often pick up the wrong hen and wring its neck. Since he had been in her service for decades, she couldn't bring herself to tell him to go. Sensing her delicacy in the matter, the sweeper one day just decided to die in his sleep in the servants' quarters.

Betty taught me how to bake the perfect lemon pie. I still have the recipe that she wrote out for me in her long, loopy handwriting. Since we didn't have an oven, we would bake it by placing the aluminium tin tray on the coals, placing another tin covering on the top and putting some hot coals on that as well. Whenever I made it, it came out perfect. Besides that, she showed me how to bake a coconut pie, a sponge cake, and how to whip and mash potatoes into a smooth, creamy texture. She would sometimes bring up a plateful of cookies that she had

---

4 Mrs. Sharma, someone is throwing stones on my roof early morning these days. My sleep is ruined!

5 Mrs. Ingram, but your hens and roosters make a lot of noise in the early hours of the morning.

6 But Mrs. Sharma, they are stupid birds, what else can they do!

just baked to our house. Over a period of time, the Iron Lady and the Sharma family became rather good and caring neighbours. The day my father died, she and her *khansama* – the doddering butler, brought us dinner cooked in her house as the kitchen fires in our house would remain doused for a week, as is the custom in Hindu homes.

When it came the turn for old Mr. Ingram to pass on to the other world, he decided to do so in his sleep. This was just as well because Betty was by now quite old to run around hospitals, which in a hill station are located at places deliberately farthest from your house. Often enough, the person being taken to the hospital dies midway and saves everyone a lot of bother.

I was the first person she called to say her husband expired during the night and would I come down and help her dress him. I had, and still do, a mortal fear of handling dead bodies but how could I get out of this situation? My mother gave me the final push reminding me how helpful Betty had been when my father died. So, I summoned up my courage and went down. She was red-eyed but composed and told me that when she went to wake him up in the morning, he wouldn't stir and then she realized he had gone. She brought out a dark suit and together we somehow got him into it. She knotted the tie around his collar. When the coffin arrived, we placed him into it and then walked up the steep climb to the cemetery that was a good three miles away.

Six years later, I had to accompany my mother to Mussoorie to sort out some legal matter. I had called up Betty to say we were coming and asked her to book us into a hotel. She bent my ear on that! She would not stand for us staying at a hotel, and said there was always room for us at her house. This coming from her, a person who never really welcomed anyone but her son into her house, was the kindest gesture of all. We spent two nights with her and out of deference for her gracious hospitality, not once did I cringe or complain when the roosters crowed!

Chapter 23

Blue Murder

She had come to us as a chit of a girl just stepping into her teens. Plump, dark, pig-tailed, but with a smile that could even light up the spark in someone of a sour and surly demeanour. Always chattering nineteen-to-the-dozen, she would barely sit still and was always seen on her feet. That was tantalising Tina... jolly most of the time, yet in a flash she could also show her flip side... that of a vicious, spoilt and sharp-tongued brat.

Her father was an old friend of our father's and he had descended upon us, out of the blue one day, with his daughter in tow. Nouveau riche, but still retaining the old world charm of speech and manner, he bowled my parents over and persuaded them to allow his daughter to stay with us. Since she was joining school in mid-term, there was no way they could accommodate her as a boarder in the school my sisters attended. And so here she was, dumped bag and baggage on our doorstep and immediately accepted as part of the family. I must admit she brought a whiff of cosmopolitan Delhi into our rather staid little lives and often scandalised my sisters with tid bits about the boys from the plains.

At the start of the next school year, Tina got accepted as a boarder at the school. Secretly, we all heaved a big sigh of relief because after a month or so, she had begun to get on our nerves and had, in one way or another, managed to get on the wrong side of everyone – from our parents down to the servants. Although a big show of how we'd miss her was on display when her father again came up after the winter holidays to leave her at school, we could barely conceal our relief that this bundle of mischief was out of our hair.

Tina, surprisingly, threw a fit, jumped up and down and screamed her lungs hoarse that she did not want to go to boarding school. Much to our consternation, her father appeared quite helpless at controlling her and almost appeared to succumb to her theatrics. But my mother, sensing that he was about to cave in, immediately suggested that Tina could always come home on weekends to us. That stopped her tantrum and she agreed, once she had been cajoled enough by her father.

Thrice, Tina ran away from the boarding school and landed up at home. Once she showed up at around eight o'clock at night, which is like four in the morning in the hills. Frantic calls from the school would be made each time she bolted and my father would have a hell of a time reassuring the authorities that she would not do it the next time. Every weekend, she would trot home with my sisters. The nuns had agreed to this arrangement as they, I suppose, had also found Tina too much to handle 24/7. Of course, the donation her father had given to the school no doubt helped!

On weekends at home, Tina would doll up whenever we went to town on our evening walks. My sisters, who were not allowed to wear makeup at that young age, were first aghast, and then turned all giggly until Tina silenced them with a withering look. Soon, she began encouraging them to also experiment with lipstick and mascara. But one sharp word from my mother was enough to send them scurrying to wash it off their faces. So, Tina remained the undisputed glamour girl.

Since Tina still had enough years to go before she would pass out of school, her parents rented a house close to the Mussoorie Club. Every summer, they would take residence here and Tina would then, naturally, become a day scholar for that period and stay with them. Since schools in Delhi would close for two months for the summer holidays, her two brothers and younger sister would also be there.

The Club, during the evenings, would actually function as a gambler's den. Round tables would be requisitioned for men and women addicted to their daily session of cards. Waiters would bring the drinks and snacks to their tables. Among the raised bids of Flush and tense moments of Rummy and Bridge, children would weave in and around the tables plucking the snacks off their parents' plates. On weekends, the Club would organise Housie, a favourite pastime with young and old alike. This also served as a fashion parade of sorts for the young boys and girls, besides an occasion to flirt discreetly in public. A couple of love affairs blossomed during the games of Housie and led to dates at the skating rink where the couple could clasp hands while roller skating to the music.

However, what was happening to our Tina in all this feverish, seasonal cooing and wooing? Tina was also blossoming and feeling the sexual heat that the hot summer generated among the pimply youth. Quick to scent this was a flashy, middle-aged rake by the name of Mahesh who turned up every season to line his pockets with winnings from the gambling tables at the Club. He wormed his way to the table dominated by Tina's mother who behaved like, and vaguely reminded one of, a vamp from the silver screen. By allowing her to win a couple of times, he gained her favour, as well as an entry into their house. Tina's father, a genial old man quite besotted with his gaudy but glamorous wife, was just as taken in by the young gambler and would often toss a few pegs with him before they sauntered down to the Club for their card game.

Roses, chocolates, perfume, along with liberal doses of flattery will usually win a young girl's heart. And Tina did not prove to be an exception. The rake had managed to lure her with his wiles and guiles; she had been blinded by his flash and dash. He, on the other hand, was looking to ensnare the daughter of fairly wealthy parents and the nubile Tina, although a very plain looking lass, sans make up, seemed easy prey. It was later rumoured that he was rather neck deep in debt and the creditors were on his back. So, this season he was gambling for more than just petty winnings to pay for his lodge and board in some sleazy hotel in Mussoorie. He was gambling for his survival.

They had begun to meet clandestinely. One rainy evening, while the parents were at the Club playing cards, Mahesh slipped into their house. Tina, who had been expecting him, had left the front door ajar and was preparing coffee in the kitchen. Soaked to the skin as he was, she got him to remove his shirt. He came closer and wrapped her in his arms. Suddenly, her brother, who was around nine, ran into the kitchen and froze seeing both of them in a compromising position. In a flash, Tina grabbed a kitchen knife and threatened him saying, "*Agar mummy aur daddy ko kucch bola toh dekhna phir mein kya karoongi!*"[1]

The situation rapidly escalated. Chintu tried to run out the door; Mahesh grabbed him by the arms; Tina, livid, furious and scared out of her wits, suddenly lunged and plunged the kitchen knife into Chintu's belly. Mahesh ran down to the Club to fetch her parents.

Half an hour or so after the incident, my father got a call at home. It was Tina's father asking him and my mother to rush straight to their home, above the Club. The boy had been rushed in a critical condition to the hospital where, some hours later, he succumbed to the fatal wound.

---

[1] If you tell mummy or daddy anything then you see what I will do to you!

In a small town like ours, things are easily hushed up. Besides the families involved, the doctor and the police inspector, I doubt anyone else heard of this *crime de passionel* – a murder most foul. A story was concocted about the whole incident. The servant was paid handsomely to take the blame and confess to accidentally stabbing the boy who had stormed into the kitchen demanding to be fed. I heard he was out of the prison within a year. The rake slipped out of the town. Tina was overnight removed from the school and whisked away to Delhi – never to be seen in Mussoorie again.

A year later, we heard she got married to Mahesh who was at least twenty years her senior. And, she showed up at our door some thirty years later... looking none the worse for wear. She had left her husband and was now footloose. That edge she had to her was still there – simmering under the surface.

Chapter 24

The Unlikely Brotherhood

They met in secret.

There was Omi, the ironmonger.

There was Gurdayal Singh, the hardware merchant.

There was Ishawari Prasad, the jalebi and sweetmeats shop-walla.

There was Captain Dayal, whose title was purely honorary, conferred by the British on his late father, and usurped rather unceremoniously by the aging son.

There was Swaroopi, the manager of a boarding and lodging place.

There was Bishamber, the local doctor.

There was my father – a gentleman of leisure. And then, there were others.

These were the so-called Freemasons of Mussoorie!

While crossing each other on the Mall Road or sitting around a card table at the Mussoorie Club, they would, through various hand-signs or maybe twitches of their eyes or ears, convey the day and time of their next meeting.

My mother, of course, always knew when the next meeting was scheduled because my father would have a distinct sparkle in his eyes and would be fidgety all day long, waiting for the moment he could leave the house. She knew that, that day she would be resigned to spending an evening with her hen group, playing rummy, or with us children for company. She always preferred the former.

The Masonic Club, as it was popularly called, was formally known as 'Lodge Dalhousie 1854 of Mussoorie and Deyrah' and was located in a rather mysterious looking, single-storey bungalow atop the Picture Palace Bus Stand. One never saw a living soul moving around in its grounds. Not during the day, at least! There was no sign of any chowkidar or caretaker either. Yet, it always looked rather spruce and well maintained. It commanded a grandstand view of the lush Doon Valley below.

Once, I went along with a friend to snoop around the Lodge in the late afternoon. Since I had a missionary school back-ground, I was quite familiar with the story of King Solomon and vaguely remembered his connection to the Guild of Masons that his father-in-law, King Hiram of Tyre, is credited with having established. We peeked through its glazed windows but could see nothing but some dark brown woodwork. I was disappointed. I had expected to catch a glimpse of huge candelabras, incense burners, swords and other ritualistic paraphernalia. There was nothing to be seen.

Yet, there were plenty of stories and rumours one heard about the Lodge.

Some people said that the men who belonged to the Brotherhood met just for drunken revelries and cavorted around nude in rituals that involved black hoods, swords, large tapered candles and huge pentagrams chalked on the floor. Others gossiped about bordello-like bedrooms and said they had seen flashily dressed women (certainly not from Mussoorie;

perhaps from the Doon valley, down below) enter the gates of the Lodge, well past midnight. And some townsfolk hinted that it was really a 'no-women allowed' area and that the men gathering there were engaging in buggery and all manner of otherwise forbidden activities that were essential ingredients of their rituals and rites. Be that as it may, there were no reliable eyewitnesses to the goings-on at the infamous Lodge.

So, what did the Brotherhood do for the town or the townspeople for that matter, by way of improving the infrastructure, water supply or even supporting some philanthropic projects? They did zilch. Anyway, what would money-grubbing traders, vegetable and sweetmeat vendors, ironmongers and the like know about the ideals of the real Masonic brotherhood? Zilch, again, I think. How, and on what basis, they got invited to join the Lodge was perhaps the biggest mystery, even more mysterious than the rumoured secret initiation rites of the Brotherhood.

When strolling on the Mall Road alongside my father, which in itself was a fairly rare occurrence, I would keep my eyes peeled out whenever I would spot a suspected fellow Mason coming from the opposite side. I strained hard to see if my father would make some kind of subtle hand sign like the deaf use to communicate. But, I never saw him shake a fist, furtively open and close his palm, or cross index and middle fingers like one does to ward off the evil eye.

Yet, there were these large group photographs of the Brothers posing at their regular annual Lodge dinners, which my father had framed and hung on the walls of his office. In these pictures, even the vegetable and sweetmeat vendors as well as the ironmonger looked like refined gentlemen, dressed in suits and wearing the Masonic regalia of ribbons and medals and other such decorations. I decently confined these by-now-yellowed photographs to the flames after about fifty years, as they were just using up precious space in my small Mumbai apartment.

What is the point of this chapter you may well ask? It's quite simple, really. According to what I have read of Freemasonry, the Brotherhood is supposed to help one another in the regular course of life, but more so in times of adversity. Yet, when my father fell on bad times, or even when he suddenly died of cardiac arrest in the middle of the road, I don't recall any of the so-called 'Brotherhood' coming forward, secretly or openly, to offer help of any kind. The point is that most of these philanthropic institutions, I believe, function as private clubs for pleasure and mutual benefit.

Last year, I was up on a visit to Mussoorie. The Lodge still stands there looking abandoned and desolate. It hasn't changed a bit; it hasn't been sold off, and it hasn't been let out. Yet its lawns are manicured, the gravel newly spread. Someone is taking care of it. The question is – who? Now that's a mystery waiting to be solved. But I'm neither Hercule Poirot nor Sherlock Holmes.

Chapter 25

Of Casanovas, Billiard Champs, and Ladies Fair

Dev was without doubt the handsomest boy of Mussoorie. Not very well educated, but when one has good looks where's the need for brains or brawn? Dev wasn't missing them either because he was doing quite well in life, thank you, on the basis of his looks. He was slowly going places.

Handsomely fair and reasonably tall for a Garhwali boy, he had scraped through his Intermediate exam and, through the good offices of his father who was once a respected but now a discredited banker, he got an administrative job in the office of the Survey of India. Where exactly he lived in Mussoorie, I never could find out. Living on the fringes of our hill station's so-called high society, he never failed to make heads turn whenever he sauntered down the Mall, always dressed impeccably in a formal jacket and trousers creased to a knife's edge. Yes, Dev never walked, he sauntered, one hand casually pushed into the side pocket of his trousers. This was the mid-fifties and his hair, that always appeared freshly shampooed and blow-dried, swung this way and that on his fair forehead as he swaggered down a slope. Dev never sat on a railing along the Mall like the other loafer boys of the town. He just strode up and down the Mall, every evening without fail, on his way to or from the skating rink.

Known as the discredited banker's son, one would have thought Dev to constantly wear an abashed, persecuted expression. But no, he looked the world squarely in the eye as if daring anyone who would defy his look or make some caustic remark. No one ever did, at least not to his or his brother's face.

One particularly nawabi, aristocratic habit of Dev, I think, compelled people to always greet him with a fair degree of politeness and courtesy. On meeting a well-heeled member of our town out for an evening walk, he would pull his hand out of his pocket and open it, making a barely noticeable, courtly bow, to offer two or three pods of *elaichi*[1]. Now this was on offer that no one could refuse, else it would have meant showing a great discourtesy to the person offering it. I bet he did this at work too whenever officers came on inspection tours.

How many hearts he broke in Mussoorie, I was too young to know or care about. I was pleased that whenever he met me on the road, or on the skating floor, he would visibly bow, open his hand to offer a couple of elaichis, smile that slightly lopsided smile and say, "How are you, *chhotay*[2] Sharmaji?" I was not particularly fond of elaichis, but never failed to take one, so as not to offend him. Of course, Dev was merely showing me a courtesy, because somewhere at the back of his mind, he thought that perhaps one day he might need to ask my father a favour. I don't think that day ever came but Dev was always one to hedge his bets.

One summer, two Gujarati sisters landed up in our town to escape the heat and dust of the plains. Now, every tourist – young or not-so-young, rich or almost rich or just above the poverty line – would make it a point to visit the skating rink to

---

1 Cardamom.
2 Young.

gape and gawk, see and be seen, moving robot-like round and round the wooden floor of the skating rink. Evening sessions were more popular than the morning rounds because the girls and boys would come sporting the latest look and fashions that were the current rage in Bollywood. Those were the days of Asha Parekh, Sadhana, Saira Banu, among the girls, and Dharmendra, Jeetendra and Sunil Dutt, among the boys of the Hindi film industry. Each had his or her trademark look.

The richy-rich Gujarati sisters, however, were immune to the dictates of current fashion. They came wearing their expensive silk blouses, with suffocating high necklines and three-fourth sleeves, and silk saris wrapped most ungracefully about their hips; their hair properly oiled and plaited and *gajras*[3] of jasmine pinned to their plaits. On their feet would be walking shoes, totally mismatched with their attire, but perfect for the roller skates they would have to put on at the skating rink. Neither of them knew how to skate, but since they were in Mussoorie they just had to do it so they could brag about it to their friends when they went back, and so they were hell-bent on learning to roller skate.

The older sister also wore a pair of horned spectacles that only served to make her already plain features appear sterner. The younger one looked like a carbon copy. Their sexual scent was out and wafting on the summer breeze and it rolled right under Dev's flaring nostrils. So, catching the scent of his prey, Dev's wardrobe went up a notch and his courtesies became more elaborate. The quality and size of the elaichis also showed a sudden improvement! Soon, he was teaching the older sister to balance herself on the skates – not an easy job for a beginner. I saw her teeter over backwards a couple of times, but Dev's arm would quickly snake around her waist and not allow her to land on her bottom.

---

[3] Small floral garland.

Wonder of wonders! The ugly duckling now learnt to float like a swan on roller skates and soon she, and Dev in full plumage, became a regular couple skating and swaying in rhythm to the latest Hindi film songs that played on an ancient gramophone. Round and round the oval wooden floor they glided. Dev would show off his tricks by skating up the V-shaped bridge, doing a turn in the air, and then rolling down the other side backwards to the applause of the two sisters. It was a simple enough manoeuvre even I had learnt to perform, as had many of the other expert skaters. But the sisters' eyes were only on him! While Dev swirled around with the older sister, his brother partnered the younger one.

Those were not the days of email or even the mobile phone. So, how the two stayed in touch after the summer interlude was over is something I can't explain. All I know is they were back the next summer dot on May 1. This time around, they did not just meet at the skating rink. The sisters, accompanied by their brothers, cousins and parents, would be parading most mornings and evenings on the Mall. Dev, since he was working during the day, could only accompany them on their evening outing on the Mall. He seemed to have acquired a fair amount of poise and polish and a couple of new suits as well, courtesy I suppose, the generous purse of his lady un-fair. The playboy had decided enough was enough. He wasn't getting any younger; he had had enough of his clerical job and of our one Mall Road, three-rickshaw town. So he took the final plunge. Who proposed, who accepted, is still unknown. But the couple were wed and soon fled on their honeymoon.

Some romances do end up the 'Mills and Boon' way. Some fairy tales *do* have a happy ending.

Simran was the second daughter of a garrulous, old sardar who ran a small curio shop in our town. I remember Simran as the girl who wore her hair in two plaited loops on either side of her rather bony, oval face. She didn't look very pretty in her school uniform of white blouse and navy blue tunic. In fact, one hardly paid her any attention at all in those days. She was in the same class as my sister Tosh and one of her best friends.

While my sister went to a college in Delhi, Simran went on to join the Lady Fernshaw college for women in Simla. This came as a surprise to us, for the old sardar was known to keep a hawk's eye on his daughters and never let them stray too far from his home or shop – leave alone the town! Later we found that since there was no scope for higher studies after finishing school in our town, and his daughter did want to go to college, he had no choice but to allow Simran to attend college in another town. But, he first went on a recce to Simla and the college to see if it was safe and secure for young girls. The Principal of that college assured him that his daughter would be in safe custody at the hostel. Having satisfied himself that the morals and chastity of his daughter would not be compromised, he allowed her to join Ferns, as it was known.

That year, Simran won the Miss Ferns crown. Away from the stern and disapproving eye of her father, the rather timid, bird-like, beak-nosed, thin girl, seemed to have filled out and blossomed into a bird of paradise. The tid bit about his daughter having won the title was kept from the townsfolk and only came to light when Simran returned to the hills for the summer holidays. She confided in my sister that she had been crowned the winner in the annual beauty contest. And it wasn't surprising to see why, after we had got one good look at the new, improved Simran.

Gone was the well-oiled, centre-parted hair worn in two-plaits. It was now blow-dried and pushed up into the popular bouffant style of the late-fifties. She had learnt to tie her sari the way film stars tied theirs, in a hip-hugging style that showed off the curves to an advantage. When the two sisters stepped out for their evening walk on the Mall, all heads turned to take a second look at Simran as she walked past. Seeing us, the sisters would pause for a brief moment to exchange 'Hi-Hellos' and comment on the weather. All the while, Simran would keep playing with her tiny, diamond nose-ring while letting out a tinkling laugh at some juicy bit of gossip my sister had to pass on. Our interaction with the two sisters was limited to these brief meetings on the Mall Road, or to those rare occasions when we stepped into their tiny shop.

The Chinese invasion of 1962 changed all that.

Earlier, I had mentioned the patchy variety show we had put together to raise funds for the war effort. One highlight of that variety show depicted a *jawan*[4] home on furlough serenading his sweetheart in the village in a song and dance routine. Unknown that she has been betrothed to him since they were both children, the girl initially shrugs off his advances. While romping around, a thorn pierces the sole of her foot and the dashing jawan deftly pulls it out. In the course of the song, she comes to know that he is the one to whom she is to be shortly wed. Simran pranced and danced in the role of the village belle, while being serenaded by her beau to a popular Punjabi folk song. The boys from St. George's who formed a sizeable part of the audience whistled and clapped rhythmically along. It was, without doubt, one of the most popular items of the show.

Sometimes, life does imitate art. Simran too had an admirer who had diligently pursued her through her years at Fernshaw College. He was the heir apparent of a princely estate near Azamgarh. But, of course, not a breath of scandal had yet reached the ears of the puritan sardar back home. Simran had

---

4 Soldier.

hugged the secret close to her tiny bosom. Once she completed her studies, she told the prince that under no circumstances would her father agree to a union with a Muslim prince. Their worlds were poles apart – she was an ordinary shopkeeper's daughter and he a prince of royal blood. The prince however remained undeterred and persisted that his suit would have to be heard by her parents.

At her wits' end, Simran approached my sister who in turn approached our father. After all, they reasoned, hadn't our father come around to condone the marriage of his sister with the Bihari Babu? Who else would understand Simran's plight better that him, and who else would be a better ambassador to press the suit with her father? That's how a meeting was arranged. The prince drove up from his estate to Mussoorie and was invited home for high tea. Simran arrived separately, about fifteen minutes later after making some excuse to her parents. The prince declared that he would marry Simran no matter what, while Simran timorously and tearfully expressed her fear that her parents would on no condition approve of this liaison.

My father pacified both by saying he would use his good offices with her father and bring him around. The prince left that evening for Azamgarh, and my sister went to accompany Simran to her father's shop, as if they were just returning from a regular evening walk, instead of an evening of high-pitched romance and drama. It was a no-go. The hard-hearted and unrelenting sardar told my father he would never agree to this marriage and, if it came to that, he would disown her completely. Her sister pleaded, her mother sobbed, my mother begged – but the sardar remained adamant. There would be no marriage. He thus doomed his daughter to spinsterhood. He had earlier messed up his elder daughter's marriage, and had now snuffed out all hope for his younger daughter.

Ranji Mama didn't walk. He swooped like Batman when he passed you by on the Mall Road. In the winters that always set in early in Mussoorie, he would drape... drape and never wear it like normal people would... his navy-blue woollen overcoat that despite its weight would billow out like a cape, as he strode quickly down a slope. Underneath, he always wore a shirt (never a sweater) with its two top buttons undone regardless of the cold weather. The collar of the overcoat would always be upturned and his eyes would be turned down looking at his shoes as if nothing else in the world was worth his notice.

A boy who never spoke unless spoken to, Ranji Mama appeared to have stopped putting on weight as soon he turned sixteen. Now six feet tall at twenty-five, he wouldn't have tipped the scales above fifty or fifty-five kg. There was nothing remarkable about his face. He had short, black, curly hair that was already receding at the temples. His brows were usually knitted as if he was thinking about something and his button-hole, black eyes could stare at you without blinking if, by sheer luck, you were able to arrest his attention and engage him in a conversation that would in the end turn out to be one-sided. He would just say "Ahaaa" or "Hmmm" and shake his head from side to side or nod in agreement or disagreement.

I was a friend of his elder brother, Narendra, who was an avid skater. He had inherited his father's eye problem in that his left eye had a permanent cast and appeared as if it was made of glass, as it more or less remained static, while the right eye would dart this way and that. He was always seen in a blue blazer and grey trousers when he stepped out on the Mall. Even with the stonish eye, he fancied himself as a playboy who was, at least to his mind, irresistible to the opposite sex. Unlike Ranji Mama who strode and swooped, Narendra walked with precise, measured steps that made it appear as though he was strutting and not walking.

How did I come to be acquainted with Narendra who was, after all, the son of the one-eyed ticket seller at the Capitol cinema in Mussoorie and several rungs down the social ladder? Well, for one, I saw almost every movie that played at the Capitol – sometimes taking in two shows a day – the eleven o'clock English movie and the two o'clock Hindi movie. I would usually ring up the ticket seller from my home and ask him to keep a corner seat for whichever show I wanted to see. And since he called my father Panditji, he often called me Sharmaji even though I was just a skinny lad of thirteen.

Ditto his elder son, Narendra. After completing his Intermediate at the local college for boys, Narendra joined the Indian Army. The training had made his back even more ramrod straight than it had been before. Now it appeared that the army had shoved a steel rod into his arse and all the way up his back. My friendship with Narendra soon fizzled out as he was, for the better part of the year, stationed at far-off places and only came home during his annual leave.

Since I was known both to his father and his elder brother Narendra, Ranji Mama would often walk past without acknowledging me on the Mall Road. This would cheese me off no end and I thought he was either too much of a simpleton or one hell of an arrogant bugger. This attitude changed when I came to know him better. How did this seemingly impossible friendship develop between us?

In 1964, I had abandoned Law studies a week after they had begun and run home to Mussoorie primarily because I could not find accommodation at Jubilee Hall, which was the hostel for post-graduate students at Delhi University. There was another major reason why I left my Law classes but this is not the appropriate place to divulge that.

Fact is I was back at home with nothing to do but saunter idly on the Mall Road. In April next year, the Mussoorie Degree

College started post-graduate classes and I enrolled for the Master's course in English Literature. There were just five of us in the first batch of three boys and two girls. One of the boys called Raghubir was a first cousin of Ranji Mama. Since I was the only one with an English medium background, the other two boys looked up to me. The girls mostly kept to themselves.

Raghubir was a good billiard player so I drove an agreement that he would teach me billiards and I would try to improve his English. In the evenings, we would meet at the Billiard Parlour, which was above a row of shops in Kulri. Ranji Mama would arrive an hour late from his job at the Municipal Office and after I had learnt to handle the cue and pot the balls, we would make a foursome with one of the other boys and have another round or two of the game.

Mama was an even better player than Raghubir and one got to pick up good tips just by watching him play. If I was paired with him, he always showed lots of patience and admirable restraint when I knocked the ball off the table or gave an easy opening to score to the opposing pair. In a few months, he had loosened up a bit – enough to start addressing me by my pet name. Sometimes we would meet another group of boys to play volleyball in the courts of one of the hotels. Although I would be the last person to be picked by either of the teams, Mama would often do his best to see that I was in his team. I was rarely given a chance to volley the ball and usually just got to serve it. My job done, I would then just watch the other boys hit it back and forth across the net.

It was Mama who first taught me to drink and the drink was usually Old Monk Rum. I can never forget the amusement of the boys, whom I was now hanging out with, when we would walk down Taar Galli and they would stop by the country liquor shop to buy cheap liquor. When they did that, I would tell them to first let me go far enough ahead, so the shopkeeper wouldn't see me. If he had, the news would travel to my family that I was drinking country liquor and there would be hell to pay. Besides, I hated the smell of it.

Once, Mama compelled me to take a swig and I gagged and spat the stuff out. I cursed them all, much to their amusement. Once drunk, the boys would usually start singing popular songs from Hindi films. My voice, which was more soprano than contralto, would come in handy singing the female portions, if the song happened to be a duet. Gradually, I got the boys off country liquor and we would then go to some roadside bar to have a tot of rum or whiskey.

I was already smoking cigarettes but in the company of Mama, I came down from Capstan to the Charminar brand, which in those days was priced at just twenty-five paise or four annas for a pack of ten. He taught me how to blow smoke rings one evening, by giving an impressive demonstration. "Hold the smoke, pucker the mouth, suck in the cheeks, curve your tongue and blow the ring out as if you are whistling," he instructed. Later, he showed me how to blow a smaller ring through a bigger ring in quick succession.

When my father died, it was Ranji Mama who with his strong, silent support stood like a pillar by my side. He was among the first to arrive on hearing the news and I remember I was on the grounds outside the cottage. He came silently; hearing the crunching of gravel under his feet, I turned around and he, without uttering a word, just gave me a hug. He didn't offer any condolences. He prolonged his embrace and I, who never ever shed tears for anyone, just broke down for a few seconds. He, his cousin Raghubir, and a few other boys came every evening to my home to sleep for the thirteen days of the mourning period. We would all sleep together on the floor of the living room. In the morning, while I was still asleep, the boys would go to their homes and about their work.

Mama's wedding was also the first wedding I attended in my independent capacity. I found it very strange that for a Garhwali boy he didn't find a girl nearer home. Instead, the girl, who was also a Garhwali, lived in Amritsar. He insisted I come and I was able to get permission from home to go. Off I went with the marriage party by third class sleeper, to the city of the Golden Temple. That was also the first and the last time I visited the famous shrine. The wedding itself was a fairly ordinary affair and after three days we took the train back home.

Those Charminar cigarettes that he smoked finally took their toll. At the young age of thirty-five, having sired two sons, Mama contracted tuberculosis of the lungs. I had left Mussoorie long since and when I returned to it after a gap of ten years or so, my friend Ganesh broke the news that Mama had died, in his arms, at the Community Hospital in Landour, early that year. When later, much later, I was diagnosed with cancer, I, in a fit of remorse, reached out to Mama, wherever in the Heavens he may have been, to look out for me.

Mama. When sometimes my mind turns to him, I see him striding down the slope of Kulri, his blue-black overcoat swung around his shoulders and flapping like Batman's cape in the winter wind.

Gawky, golliwog-ish and Goan – that was Sandra at fifteen, the daughter of our local dispensing chemist who also ran a flourishing store that sold almost everything from cat food to chocolates and dispensed cough elixirs and other powders that cleared throat, lungs and bowels in a jiffy. The embossed plaque outside the shop bore the swirling legend of Gomes & Sons. Yes,

Sandra had two brothers – one ill fated and the other, a young rascal. The boys went to Wynberg-Allen and Sandra went to the Convent of Jesus & Mary, Waverley, where my sisters studied.

The Gomes lived at the bottom of the slope that ran from our house down to where the Mall Road ended. They couldn't have lived in a more secure place as attached to their spacious shop was the police chowky of Happy Valley. How many happy souls dwelled there is anybody's guess. My own guess is not too many... as in those early days it was inhabited largely by Anglo-Indian widowers and spinsters living out their solitary lives in a valley that was largely neglected by the sun for the better part of the day and reminded one of Thomas Hardy's dark and solitary countryside. The bungalows in which they lived were set far apart. The widowers wore tweed jackets and smoked pipes, while the ageing spinsters wore floral, ankle-length dresses and tight curls that peeked out of their hats or caps pulled over their heads. A few had rinsed their hair with blue or violet dye.

The bungalows that they haunted had typically British names – Brightwood, Falcon's Nest, Ridgewood, Windermere, Hollyhock, The Oaks, and such. As a child, I don't recall a happy sound ever emanating, leave alone echoing, in our Happy Valley. So much for inappropriately named people and places! We were on nodding terms with most of them and had a couple of times been invited to their cottages for tea and cucumber sandwiches. They were gracious but distant as the *gora logs*, or white folk, were with the brownies and *kaala aadmis*[5] in the early 1950s. It had been barely five years since Independence and it was in the fitness of things that they still clung to the airs and graces of their Raj days.

The Gomes fell between two stools. Neither were they fair and pink-cheeked like the Anglos, nor were they desi enough to be accepted as fellow Indians, although they were as brown

---

[5] Dark skinned natives.

as acorns. Yet, they were a cheerful family. Mrs. Gomes always, and I mean always, had a kettle simmering over her stove that sat plonked in the centre of her chintz-curtained drawing room. Spring, summer, winter, it always felt pleasantly warm and stuffy. While Shilton, the elder son, slept in the tiny cottage behind the shop, Mikey, the young rascal chose to sleep in a bedroom behind the shop separated by just a two-foot pathway from the family's cottage. While the rest of the family slept soundly in the cottage, Mikey would sneak out and hobnob with the policemen in the chowky to smoke a *beedi* – crushed tobacco rolled in a tobacco leaf, to get an update on the gossip doing the rounds of not just Happy Valley, but the entire hill station of Mussoorie.

This story however is not about the Gomes family. It is about Sandra. Now, Sandra, like most Christian girls of the day, had a tightly curled, permed head of hair that haloed around her face and was quite the envy of my elder sister, who had long, Rapunzel-like plaits that she wore in loops tied with ribbons around the sides of her head. Yes. Her hair was really long and hung down to well below her waist when she opened her plaits. Our granny loved her hair, so it was no wonder that she threw a fit and a faint the day my sister, in conspiracy with our father and mother, quietly went one day to Mavis – the hairdresser of the Anglo-Indian ladies of the town.

The three of them came home at night, with my sister sporting a permed head of hair just like Sandra's. For a minute, we couldn't recognise her. My grandmother first squinted her eyes, and then they kept widening as she gazed in horror at my sister. Then she pointed a shaking finger at my mother and said, "You-you-youuu... how could you let her cut off her lovely hair... you want her to look like those *achoot*[6] Anglo-Indian girls?" And turning to my father, she said, "You are the bigger fool," and slapping the palm of her hand to her forehead, she muttered,

---

6 Untouchable.

"This is what comes of sending your girls to schools run by those crow-like women," meaning the nuns in their black habits.

Although she looked like a golliwog, I have to admit the new hairdo suited her and she looked rather like a Memsahib. The next year, the one younger to her went and got her hair cut and permed. So now there were two golliwogs. The third one would follow in their footsteps a few years down the line. All three would adopt the same hairstyle.

Sandra admired my elder sister's thick, lush curls. Her own were like tiny wire springs. Since my second sister and I would initially keep taunting and calling the elder one a golliwog, she and Sandra hatched a plan to torment us.

It so happened that a shortcut to our school led by the side of a graveyard in which a few nuns and, perhaps, one or two priests lay buried. While taking this path occasionally, we would always hurry past the graveyard; in case one of the dead nuns came flapping out to cart us away. In fact, this was the story circulated by the teachers and the other hired help at the school. Even our old chowkidar, Bishna, swore that two young goatherds whom he knew had been swooped upon by these dead nuns and carted away inside the graveyard from which they never reappeared. Presumably, they also had turned into ghosts.

Contrary to popular belief, the residents of this graveyard never sauntered out at midnight, which is the usual hour for ghosts to sally forth. The ones buried here were said to roam the forest in the late afternoon, just when our school would get over and we would be going home from school. Then one day, when we were passing the 'spot' where the shortcut to the graveyard met the main road, we began to hear wails and shrieks and cackles of wicked laughter. We arrived home with ashen faces. Our mother noticed that I had wet my shorts and my younger sister was teary-eyed and inquired what was wrong. Had our teachers punished us for something we had done? She probed and she probed and drew the story of the diabolical ghosts from us.

The next day, she instructed that we wait in the school until the servant arrived to bring us home. That day, and the day after that, nothing happened. No ghostly rustlings in the trees, no wailing. Sandra and my elder sister had probably decided to take a break lest they were caught. On the third day, the servant could not come to pick us up. So the 'ghosts' got up to their tricks again. But this time, my sister caught a glimpse of one of them and told my mother that the ghost wore a school uniform and she thought that there were two ghosts. Well, the next day our mother, without informing anyone, stood at that cursed place waiting for us around a bend in the road.

As she heard our approach, she saw a rustling in the bushes overhead and spied two girls as they began to shake the branches of the bushes and let out wails interrupted by cackles of maniacal laughter. She told us to run home while she dealt with the ghosts of the dead nuns. A few minutes later, she came down the slope accompanied by our elder sister and Sandra, grabbing them by the collars of their blouses. "Here are your two chudails," she said, "Don't worry; they won't haunt you any longer." She warned the two girls that if they got up to their tricks again, she would immediately report them to the Reverend Mother of the school.

Now, right from the time she was in Eighth Standard, Sandra had an ardent admirer in a local shop owner who managed a very fancy, high-end department store. We used to call him 'toothpick' because he looked like one. Every evening, this young Casanova would leave the shop in the care of his father and deck himself up in a dark suit and a striped tie. Walking stick in hand, which he bandied about rather elegantly, he would stroll down the Mall towards Charleville in Happy Valley. He would step into the shop of Gomes & Sons on the pretext of buying something, hoping to catch a glimpse of Sandra, who sometimes would be there helping her father in the shop. Then, without a word, he would quietly slink out and strut back all the way to his shop.

This silent courtship went on for over a decade. Although everyone in Mussoorie, from the rickshaw puller to the Raja to the sister of the beau, was aware of the affair, Sandra's dad and her beau's dad seemed blissfully ignorant and unaware of it. Such is the blind spot that parents adopt towards their children. After completing her schooling, Sandra went off to faraway Kasauli[7] to do her teacher's training, while her beau would periodically land up there as well and woo her with chocolates and roses. This is where I think the romance took a serious turn.

Finally, after twenty years of furtively exchanged glances and coy smiles, of clandestine meetings, and after refusals of marriage proposals from other eligible bachelors and blushing brides by both the principal characters; of breast-beating and laments on the part of the parents – they two decided to elope and get married in a *gurudwara*[8] in Dehradun. Sandra renounced her faith at the gurudwara and came back in a salwar-kameez, outfitted like a *pucca sardarni*[9], now officially called Mrs. Singh.

This I think was the second inter-racial marriage in our small town after the short-lived wedding of Dorothy and Mr. Rawat. This one, however, despite its ups and downs weathered them all and is still one of the blissfully happy unions to have blossomed in Mussoorie.

---

[7] Kasauli is a cantonment and town, located in Solan district in the Indian state of Himachal Pradesh.

[8] Sikh temple.

[9] True blue Sikh woman.

Chapter 26

Nowhere to Go

If it weren't so serious, it would be hilarious! Having just graduated out of High School from Vincent Hill, with good grades (I guess 3 As, 3 Bs and 2 Cs qualify as good), I suddenly found every door to higher studies bang shut in my face. In his enthusiasm at having the only Indian child in a school full of white Americans, my father had apparently forgotten to find out if the Graduation Diploma of this school was worth the paper it was printed on! After I brought it home, we suddenly found it wasn't worth even the ink expended on it. The situation we were presented with now was - go to America, which was financially out-of-the-question, or appear for another exam in six month's time that would be recognised by the Indian education system.

In those days, there was only Matriculation at one end of the scale of education and Senior Cambridge at its other end. Matric Pass, as it was called, was strictly for the vernacular boys and looked down upon by the upper crust Indian colleges. I would have rather died than be called Matric Pass! Senior Cambridge, because of its far higher standards, was the acme of education more suited for boys belonging to the higher economic strata.

There was no option. It was decided that I would have to sit for the Senior Cambridge exams in four months. My joy at having finished with school fizzled out pretty fast. In fact, within a week, as I was loaded with new books on new subjects to study. Indian History for heaven's sake! After I had spent two years studying American History for the American School Programme! And Hindi too, which I had left behind in the Fourth Standard at Waverley convent to study French for the next four years at my Seventh Day Adventist Missionary School. Would you say it was poetic justice or injustice?

Tutors were engaged. A few came home to teach, while I had to go to the homes of others to be taught. Theorems and equations had to be revisited, Harappa and Mohen-jo-daro again excavated. Hindi was not too much of a problem, thanks to weekly releases of new Hindi films every week at the town's three cinema halls. Although my heart was not in it, I had to put my mind to it. My former school Principal had done a bit of digging and asking around and found that there was a clause that would allow them to propose and forward my name to the Cambridge Board as an examinee, that year. I was accepted and, wonder of wonders, the centre allotted to me was Waverley, the school where I had studied up to the Fourth Standard. This meant that I would be catching up with all the girls I had left behind in Standard Four and who would now also be sitting for the Senior Cambridge exam. So I would be meeting Tara, Jill, Padmini, Pramila and the others after a gap of seven years!

And guess what? By another quirk of fate, I would be the only boy sitting for the exam in a hall full of girls! First time around, it had been a case of being the only brown loaf in a bakery of white breads. This time around, it was being the only cock in a brood of hens. The Principal at Waverley hadn't changed in all these years. When I went to collect my roll number for the exam, she peered half over and half through the glasses resting midway on the bridge of her pert, Irish nose and rasped in a voice as dry as the leaves of autumn, "So, you are back with the girls again! Well, well... what on earth was your father thinking of when he put you into that Yankee school? Hadn't I told him to send you to our brother school, St. George's down at Barlowganj? Things wouldn't have come to such a sorry pass if he had heeded my advice at that time!"

Here, she paused and clicked her rosary beads, pushed her glasses higher up her button nose with a finger smeared with a blot of ink, and continued, "Well, well... best you run along now to the head clerk and collect your roll number... and, remember, no sneaking in chits into the examination hall." I blushed, stammered and stuttered something and fled from her office, remembering to dip my fingers into the 'holy water' that lay in a cupola fixed to the wall of her office, hurriedly making the sign of the cross with it.

The Senior Cambridge exams would last a fortnight. I arrived on the morning of the first paper with two Doric fountain pens, a bottle of Quink, and a stack of blotting paper. Shrieks and hoots of laughter greeted me as I entered the examination hall.

"Hey, you got the wrong centre or what? What are you doing back in the girls' school?" screamed a delighted Jill.

Tara, whose mouth was perpetually open and who spoke as if she always had marbles in it, said, "Hi... My-yy... haven't you grown!" Eight years ago, she had scribbled in my autograph book – "My heart is like a cabbage divided into two, the leaves I give to others but my heart I give to you." Childish nonsense, but it all came back in a rush.

Pramila of the saucer eyes, rolled hers as if she would faint and said, "So, you think you are going to do better than us in the exam? Haw-haw..." Pads, the princess from that tiny hill state, who back then used to be my partner in PT, raised her lowered eyes and half-whistled through the gap in her two front teeth, "Nyi-cchhe to shee you back with us."

"Hi, girls, one'n all... it feels great to be back with you!" I shot
back at them, attempting a swagger that didn't quite come off,
and a bravado that sounded a bit hollow even to my ears. "Wanna
bet who gets the most As and Bs?" Collectively, they sniggered,
winked at one another and snorted with suppressed laughter.
I think girls snort more often than boys while laughing.

At that moment, the Mother Superior rushed in. Clapping
her hands, she "Shusshhed" us all and said, "Sit down on
your seats, girls!" At this, those stupid girls again snorted with
laughter and pointed towards me. "Oh, err-rr... yes-yes, this
boy here as well... Now, we just have time for a quick prayer...
may Jesus and Mary be by your side and hold your hand as you
write your papers..." The invigilator, who had arrived, stood by
the door politely and allowed her to finish her prayer. Then he
cleared his throat to get her attention, and she whirled around
to gush, "Ah, there you are Mr. Malhotra... I leave my charges
now in your... ahem... charge." She then turned once again to
face us, made a sweeping sign of the cross in the air, and in a
pirouette of swirling black waltzed out of the hall.

The invigilator was the Principal of some vernacular school
in faraway Landour. He was a tall, thin but sprightly man, with
a pencil moustache and a rather kindly air. Year in and year out,
he sported a houndstooth tweed jacket. I cannot say whether he
possessed more than one such jacket, or whether he had three
or more in varying shades, but then they must have all been of
the same design. He would allow us to keep writing five or ten
minutes above the scheduled time for handing in our papers.

The Art paper, which was the last, was particularly messy.
It required us to do a watercolour in a certain size from a list
of five alternative choices. We showed each other our finished
paintings, which still hadn't quite dried in the cold November
of that winter, before handing it in. I wonder if they let them
dry overnight before packing them in, or just packed them in

half-wet and thereby smudged, to be air-mailed to Cambridge University in UK.

That was one of the longest winters in my memory. I don't remember doing anything of significance in the three months that followed. Did I make a short trip down to Delhi to visit my *maasi*, that is my mother's sister, who was a teacher at a public school? I can't recall. The Senior Cambridge results came out in mid-April and well, I had passed with a First Division. My father couldn't quite contain his pride and joy and proceeded to invite the Who's Who and also the Who-could-be-Who in the possible future, to lavish dinner parties. Since everyone couldn't be accommodated in our fairly large dining room with a table that could seat twenty-four people at one time, it was decided that three separate parties would be held over the coming three weeks. While the Indian part of the menu would be cooked at home, the Savoy Hotel would cater the continental fare, and the Chinese fare would be catered by Mr. Sun of the Kwality Restaurant in Kulri. Diamond Wines would send over crates of Old Smuggler and Johnny Walker Red and Black Label Whiskey.

White damask tablecloths were specially ordered from Hamer & Sons, as was a special 36-piece cutlery set from somewhere I don't remember. Rice grains, dyed in all shades of the rainbow, came in large paper bags. These were to be used to make decorative borders along the edges of the damask tablecloths. Tiny mounds of the colourful rice were also to be placed between the silver food warmers. This exercise had to be repeated three times over and, by the end of it, the children who were doing the decorating got quite sick of it. I don't remember if printed invitations were sent out or people were invited in person over phone calls. No matter, the parties were a resounding success and the guests would go back tipsy and belching from the rich repast.

What irked me the most was that none of the guests seemed to have any sense about why the parties were being held in the first place, which was to celebrate my passing with flying colours in the exam. Not a single invitee came bearing any gift for me! They all came empty handed to eat, drink and make merry. Shocking, I thought, disgusted at their lack of etiquette and lack of social graces. Not a single fountain pen, a leather-bound notebook, a shirt, a pair of cuff links, or even an envelope containing a token gift of money! Misers all! Well, most people are just not to the manner, forget the manor, born!

Armed with my mark sheet, I wrote for the prospectus of three colleges in Delhi and as soon as they arrived, filled out the admission forms and sent them back pronto through what was the only way then – by dropping them into the red letter box of the Savoy Hotel post office. A personal warning was given to the clearing postman. If he removed the stamps pasted on the envelopes, he would be sure to get a solid pasting and a dismissal from service. The calls for personal interviews came within two weeks. I bussed down to Delhi, gave my first interview at St. Stephen's College, where the Principal after asking just my name, my school's name and where I came from, handed me back my mark sheet and stamped 'ACCEPTED' on my admission form which was lying under his bespectacled nose, and told me to go and pay my fees at the registration window. That was it.

Three Mussoorie boys took admission into St. Stephen's that year. Okay, they were not strictly Mussoorie boys. What I mean is that we had gone to school together at Waverley and been together there up to Standard Four, after which we had gone to separate schools. Much like a pre-wedding bachelor party, one of the boys had a school leaving-cum-pre-college joining party at his residence, to which he had also invited a few girls who were already studying at Miranda House in Delhi.

Since my sister was already in her second year at Miranda and knew two of these girls, she was also invited to the party. As parties go, this one was a bit tacky but the girls did give us some sidelights into St. Stephen's college and what we could expect there. We three Mussoorie boys, who had never held a girl's hand, leave alone hold her in a dancer's embrace while doing the fox trot or waltz, were rather awkward and gawky at it. But the girls were good sports and told us not to be too scared and fidgety; that they were not going to eat us up. "Hey! Wipe your clammy palm and hold my hand properly... and stop trembling while you dance," one of them hissed venomously at one of the boys. I took to the safer jiving, after all rock-n-roll was the current hot dance and one didn't really need to have the girl clinging on to the entire length of your body.

One of the girls, Romila Balsaver, who was senior to my sister at Miranda House, loudly declared, "This boy here (meaning me) dances the best among you lumpkins... I think he will be a big hit with the Delhi girls!" I flushed painfully in embarrassment. That night, tossing and turning in my bed, I fantasised about the bevy of girls who would start chasing me as soon as I set foot in Delhi. Little did I know how ironic, and how totally inaccurate, Romila's prediction would turn out to be.

The college prospectus specified a list of things to be brought by each aspiring Stephanian to the hostel:

- 4 pairs of white trousers
- 6 white underwear
- 6 pairs of white socks
- 2 white shirts
- 1 dozen white handkerchiefs
- 1 pair of black shoes
- 1 cotton mattress
- 1 pillow
- 1 table fan (there were no ceiling fans in the hostel)

These were packed in a big, black aluminium trunk with my name in white enamel painted on it. The mattress and pillow and blanket went into a khaki holdall. There they sat in a corner of my bedroom – grim reminders of the fact that I would, now onwards, be left to fend for myself in a world of hostile hostelites.

It was a frightening thought and it scared the hell out of me.

Chapter 27

Doomsday

A lot like the doomsday prophets predicting the world's end in 2012, a catastrophic event had been announced in 1960. The newspapers had a field day running banner headlines proclaiming the end of the world on July 12, 1960, but my heart began to sink a fortnight before the prophecy was to come true. As the days raced towards the day I would be leaving home for the first time to join college in Delhi, I began having major apprehensions and turned increasingly morose. However, the very thought of being sneered at for my cowardice by my father or sisters made me bottle up those feelings within myself.

Fortunately, both my elder sisters were also making the trip to Delhi with me. The eldest would be flying from Delhi to resume her job as an air hostess in Bombay, while the second was looking forward to her last year at the Delhi University. The next morning, we were dropped off at the Mussoorie bus depot and put into the bus that would take us to Delhi.

It was the 11th of July, one day short of doomsday, and reaching Delhi at 7 pm that day, we went to stay overnight at our maasi's place at Jangpura. The next day, Mohinder, one of my friends in Delhi, came over to pick us up for a movie and lunch, after which they all decided to give me a grand farewell by accompanying me to the gates of my college. By this time, my heart had plummeted and sunk permanently into the pit of my stomach and I was quiet all through the forty-five minute ride to the campus.

The taxi halted at the college gates at 7.45 pm. The time stipulated for new boys to register their arrival at the hostel was no later than 8 pm. My friend helped lug out the bedroll and the trunk from the taxi's dickey and my sisters got out cheerily wishing me good luck. Reading my forlorn expression, they said, "Come on, cheer up, the world hasn't ended and we think you will survive," and asked my friend to accompany me to my room while they patiently waited at the gate. My friend picked up the roll of bedding and I picked up my trunk. Not a soul was in sight. I went to the clerk's office, checked out the block and room number that was allotted to me, and we trudged down the long corridors towards a block named Allnut South. The trunk I was carrying kept banging against the sidewalls of the narrow corridor that was lit by one faint bulb hanging nakedly from a wire. The entire block was eerily quiet and it seemed that besides the two of us, there was no one living or breathing behind the shut doors that lined the corridor on either side.

Peering at the doors as we passed them, we finally arrived at the one marked A-6. I drew the latch and entered. A bare cot woven with *newar* (broad strips of rough cotton) was lined up against one wall, a desk against another and a chair nearby. The doors of a built-in cupboard stood slightly ajar. Mohinder switched on the light and I sat down on the bed. He gave me a quick hug and said, "Acchha, I better run... the girls are waiting outside in the dark; don't worry, everything will be alright," and left me.

I collapsed and lay down on the bare bed. In the dim light of the bulb, my eyes scanned the ceiling. No fan. It was warm and humid but I was far too drained out to summon up the energy to open the trunk and take out the table fan I had brought with me.

"Sweat and suffer," I said to myself. Moving on to my side, my eyes dragged along the floor and came to rest at what looked like faded paan stains splashed in two spots. While I was wondering why no one had cleaned them, someone knocked on my door.

"Shit!" I said to myself, "Ragging at this hour, without even giving a chance for a bloke to catch his breath and settle down?"

However, I asked in a quavering voice, "Who is it?"

"Please open your door. I am your Block tutor."

I got up and unlatched the door. Standing before me was a tall, fair, bespectacled man of about thirty-odd years. He looked around the room, smiled, and said, "You should unpack and spread out your bedding. Do that, then come up to the first floor and see me."

I sighed, got up, unpacked my bedroll and spread it out on the bed without removing the mattress or the bed sheet. It would do for tonight, I thought to myself.

Then, with a heavy heart, I climbed the steps to the first floor and knocked on the tutor's door. "Come... come in," he said with a broad smile, "Did you have dinner in the mess?" he enquired. I said I hadn't and I wasn't hungry. He smiled some more and asked, "Would you like a cup of tea or coffee?" I opted for coffee. Then he sat opposite me and proceeded to ask me basic questions like where I had come from, which school I had attended, and so on.

A knock on the door interrupted his pleasant interrogation and he got up to open it to greet a senior boy who was returning home from the holidays. "Rajan, so you are back! How were your holidays?" he asked the boy. "Fine, Sir, how were yours?" he asked out of courtesy. "Rajan, can you please go down and check if Jogi has checked into the hostel and if he has, please send him up right away." The boy nodded and left. After about five minutes, another knock rapped on the door and the tutor called out, "It's open, come right in!"

He didn't walk... he shuffled. And he did that with his feet angled outwards, somewhat like a duck's. That's the first thing I noticed about him. The second thing I noticed was that he walked with his shoulders drooping and his limbs dangling loosely; his posture was not quite erect. The third thing was that he had a very Rajput-ish type of moustache. The fourth was that his eyes were rather big, reddish, and slanted upwards at the corners. That he was the scion of a princely family, I only learnt some three months later. The tutor made the introductions and then, turning to this senior boy, said, "Thakur, I would like you to watch out for him (meaning me)... he is in Room 6..."

"Do you mean A-6, Sir?" the boy's eyes widened as he exclaimed. "But that room hasn't been allotted for the last two years!" The tutor held up his index finger in some kind of a warning and stuttered, "Well, er-rr yes," replied the tutor, "but the Dean and I thought it can't be kept vacant forever, so it was decided that it should be occupied from this year onwards."

The boy shook his head and shrugged his shoulders, "Okay, Sir... may I go now?" And turning to me, he said, "I will see you later."

Soon after he left, I also went down to my room and lay on my bed waiting with some trepidation for the Gestapo-like midnight knock and some gang of seniors to come pounding on my door. Surprisingly, no one bothered me that night. Maybe the seniors were still to arrive in full strength at the hostel. The next morning, not really knowing what to do, I skipped breakfast. I tried to mingle with the two freshmen who were also in my block and went with them to get the lay of the land. We checked out our lecturers and our classrooms and generally moved around like a miserable lot dreading the gang of raggers who would shout and hoot whenever they spied timorous freshmen rounding a corner or crossing the lawn. However, this is not an ode to college life. It is in remembrance of love's labour lost... found... and lost again.

The first term was coming to an end. I patted myself on the back for having survived and lived through the torments of ragging unlike three other freshers who had, within a few weeks of the term, left the college and the hostel and gone back to their homes. I had also continued to occupy my room A-6 even after I had been told by some of the seniors why that room had stayed locked for the past two years. The boy staying in it had committed suicide by consuming a bottle of poison and his body had not been discovered for almost three to four days.

So now, the reason for the curious brown stains splashed on the floor and those still faintly peering through the hastily overpainted wall, against which my bed was placed, was clear. But somehow it didn't bother me too much. After the sordid tale came to light, some boys would occasionally joke whether his ghost came and slept alongside me at night. The fact that somewhere in my jellyfish-like timid nature I had nerves of steel, was to pull me through many difficult situations later in life.

What a joy it was to board the bus for Mussoorie the morning after the term ended! The previous night, the senior boys, occupying the row of rooms opposite mine, had thumped my back and congratulated me for pulling through the rough first term. They said I better be back after a fortnight for the second term, or else! At home, the days seemed to fly! And, before I knew it, I was back in the rickety blue bus rolling down the hills towards Delhi.

It was October and the cold weather had set in rather early. By the time I reached the hostel, it was after eight. Dumping the bag in my room, I knocked on Rangi's door and a chorus of voices yelled, "*Abay chutiye, saale... andar aa ja....*"[1] I wasn't

---

1 Come in you bloody fucker, whoever you are!

surprised to see most of our group gathered there and passing around bottles of beer. Jogi, who was huddled in a corner with one of the boys, gave me a lopsided smile, shrugged his trademark shrug and said, "Find yourself a place to squat." We were all exchanging snippets about our holiday, except for one or two of the boys who had chosen to stay back in the hostel for the term break.

"Hey guys, listen to this," yelled Chandy, the tallish boy from Kerala who lived in a block far from ours, "Suresh here had his cherry plucked this term break!" Suresh, sitting next to him, went from pink to red in the face and almost wet his pants out of sheer embarrassment. To add to it, one of the boys called Niranjan asked, "Who took your cherry Suresh... was it your cousin Sonu, or the neighbourhood boy Dinesh whom you have a crush on?"

It was way past midnight and soon everyone began to stagger off to their individual rooms.

My first winter in Delhi would prove to be a memorable one for several reasons.

I was asleep one night when around twelve-thirty, someone started thumping on my door with his fist while whispering, "Wake up, wake up, open your door... open your door! I'm feeling sick, open your door!"

"Who's there?"

"Open *yaar*[2], hurry!"

I faintly discerned that it was the voice of Jogi, my protector from the room opposite mine, and slid the latch and opened the door a crack, but he leaned forward and pushing it open, almost fell upon me. As I steadied him, I realised he was drunk to the gills and could barely stand straight.

---

[2] Friend.

"Sshhhh!" he slurred, putting a finger to his lips. "Don't make a noise... take the keys from my pocket and open the lock on my door. I can't get it to open..." saying which he almost slid to floor, as I quickly shoved my hand under his armpit to pull him up. I leaned him against the wall, opened his door and then sliding an arm around him, I half-walked, half-dragged him to his room, turned on the light and put him down on the bed.

"Put out the light... put out the light! Are you mad or what? Someone will see, so don't make any noise!" he rasped. I killed the light and said, "Hang on; I'm going to get you some water." I picked up his glass from the side table, rinsed and filled it with water from the bathroom tap and dashed back with it. "Here," I said, propping him up with one arm and putting the glass to his lips, "drink some water, you will feel better."

"Aarrgh-hh..." he grunted, took a few sips, and fell back on the bed pulling me down along with him. I somehow managed to save the glass from crashing on the floor and fell awkwardly on him. As I tried to straighten myself, he wrapped his strong arms around me in a clinch. "Stop struggling,' he murmured, "What are you scared of?" and planted his hot, dry lips on mine.

"Hey man, stop it... let me go... come on man," I protested.

"Ssshhhh," he muttered putting his finger on my lips, "Keep quiet or Rangi will hear in the next room! Okay, okay... stop the fuss, but first promise you will stay here... I'm feeling awful, really sick...," saying which he suddenly lurched up and spewed mouthfuls of whiskey-laced vomit on me.

I took his towel that was lying thrown in a corner of the room, wet it in the bathroom and came back to wipe his face and chest. I got him out of his shirt, threw it in a corner, and pulling a fresh vest from his cupboard somehow managed to slip it on him. Then I ran to take a shower myself. One of the boys came out of an adjoining room to piss and hearing the shower running asked, "What the f**k, who's left the shower running?"

He pushed open the door that I had not thought necessary to latch at that time of the night and said, "Good heavens Shiv... are you crazy taking a shower at 2 am?"

"Jeez, Nikhil," I muttered, "Shut the door, its cold... I just messed myself and came to clean up. Why can't they install geysers in here! I'm done anyway; you carry on and get to sleep." As soon as the light was switched off in his room, I dried myself and went back into Jogi's room to check if he was okay. He still had his shoes on, so I removed those along with his socks, and then pulled up a chair close to his bed and sat down on it. Once he started snoring and appeared to be sound asleep, I quietly slipped back to my room.

Neither of us mentioned or referred to the incident again. It had happened and that was it. But that was not the last of it.

Two weeks later, the same furtive knock rapped on my door. This time he was not drunk. This time he did not slur or slither. And this time I did not dither. He entered and whispered, "Move over..." and lying down beside me on the narrow cot, wrapped his arms around me. He left two hours later.

When he passed out of college, I moved out of my room and occupied his. He would drop by occasionally, sometimes in the afternoons, sometimes at night. To prevent loose talk among the other hostelites, he suggested that he would take an apartment and I should move out of the hostel and in with him since there were only a few months left now for me as well to finish college.

Two months later, holidaying with me in Mussoorie, he got a call from his house. He had been selected to join the Officers' Training School. That very afternoon he packed his bag and left. Never to be seen or heard of again.

That 'ever' was to last for the next 15 years...

Chapter 28

Law and Disorder

The years in college were somewhat of a disaster in more ways than one. Capping them was the fact that I barely scraped through the final exams and got an earful from my parents who rightly claimed that I had *paani pher diya*, in other words, 'poured water' on their hopes and dreams. That too, after having raised such high hopes during High School and in the subsequent Senior Cambridge exams.

So, what next?

"Ab kaun se papad reh gaye hain belne ko?"[1] asked my mother in a voice dripping vitriol and sarcasm. I sheepishly answered I would go back and get a degree in Law. She sneered and was proved right again when I attended just one single lecture at the Faculty of Law and never went back to the second one the next day. Instead, I caught the bus back to Mussoorie to face yet another onslaught of derision and ridicule from my dear mother.

So what did I do? In the two years that followed, I became a wastrel; loitering around on the Mall Road and whiling away evenings at the billiard rooms. Having been denied, or

---

1 Now what other disgraces are left for you to pile on our heads?

rather forbidden any contact with the local riffraff earlier, I now went all out to mingle with them and in the process found some very good friends with whom I maintain contact to this day. Back in the hills, I was, in the eyes of everyone, going downhill and gaining rapid momentum along the way. *Vela, faltu, nikkamma, kissi kaam ka nahin...*[2] were epithets that went through one ear and out of the other. Surprisingly, in all this, my father never once, not once, addressed me by any of those labels, nor did he berate me.

He was for the most part of that year away in Bareilly, overseeing some MES (Military Engineering Services) contracts that he had undertaken. When he realised I was continuously at the receiving end of these slurs and barbs, he asked me to join him in Bareilly for a few weeks. I was in Delhi at that time to see my friend Jogi off for his Officers' Training in Madras. So from there, I caught the bus one morning for Bareilly and arrived at that dusty, dirty town around seven in the evening. Over the weekend, both of us caught the train to Kathgodam and from there took a bus to Nainital, yet another hill station crowned as the Queen of the Hills. It never ceased to amaze me that almost every hill station in the North – from Uttar Pradesh to Himachal Pradesh – referred to itself as the Queen of the Hills.

Although we spent two nights in Nainital, we hardly exchanged any meaningful conversation – bonding was simply not considered and therefore totally out of question. After ten days or so, I had had enough of Bareilly and my father shoved me into a third class compartment one evening in the train bound for Dehradun. For a good two hours, I travelled standing and then requested a passenger to at least let me sit on his trunk that was blocking the passage. I still wonder why my father didn't buy me a first class ticket, but made me travel like a pig in a fart-filled sty! I guess I was no longer the Prince of Wales.

---

[2] Idler, loafer, a good-for-nothing.

In the intervening period, both my elder sisters got married to guys who were from Bombay and went their way. I think the second sister said a hurried 'yes' to a boy who my eldest sister had found, for she thought this was her best chance to escape the non-happening, stuck-in-a-time-warp (at least till then) town that held no promise of a Prince Charming coming to rescue her from it. In a way it was good to now have the house more or less to myself.

The year after that, the Mussoorie Degree College announced post-graduate courses in a few select subjects and, since I was not doing anything else, I enrolled for the Master's course in English Literature. At least, now, no one would say I wasn't doing anything and this time around I was determined to make up for the dismal performance I had put up in my B.A. in Delhi. This time I actually bought books stipulated in the curriculum and didn't skip any lectures.

In a class of five, there were only two people who could speak English fluently – a girl called Puneeta and me. The others were the so-called vernacular medium guys and why they chose English Literature for their post-graduation was hard to fathom. In between lectures, we would stand around on the terrace smoking cigarettes and looking at the under-graduate girls whose lectures began much later than ours, trudging up to college. This was the time I also realised I was getting more attracted to the fairer sex and the fairest among them happened to be the daughter of the clerk of a school for boys at Barlowganj. Tall and big built, she had a flawless peaches and cream complexion and would walk slowly and gracefully up the slope with a gait that can only be described as that of a *Gaja Gamini* that Vatsyana, in the world-famous treatise on sex called the *Kama Sutra*, likens to the walk of a she-elephant.

For a time, I was smitten by this Gaja Gamini – another 'she who walked in beauty'. She was aware of my interest in her and would sometimes come and stand alongside on the terrace deliberately allowing her dupatta to fly in the breeze and whisk across my face. I knew she came from a very conservative family and had a male cousin who was as big built as her. In the end, all it amounted to was exchanging lingering glances and occasional whisks of her colourful dupattas across my face.

Then, I almost got myself expelled the following year...

My friend Ganesh, who was going strong with a girl, had for some days fallen ill and was not coming to college. In his absence, his girl-friend and I would get together on the terrace and chitchat about how things were going between them. Her brother, who was a fresher in college that year, thought that I was getting fresh with his sister. One evening, he along with another college boy accosted me in a restaurant on the Mall where I was sitting having tea with Ganesh. He came up to our table and told me to stand up and catching hold of my collar warned me to lay off his sister. In broken English he screamed, *"I weel dree-eenk your bll-oodd... you bloody!"* He obviously didn't know the full abuse was 'bloody fool' and would only say, "You bloody." Another popular phrase was, "He is so 'proudy'"... a word that only existed in vernacular usage and nowhere in the Cambridge or Oxford dictionaries.

I was aghast. How could this lowdown creature, son of some menial clerk, dare to catch *my* collar! Anyway, my friend who was also Garhwali, intervened and said surely some mischief-makers at the college had misinformed him. So, that boy left warning me not to step foot in his locality if I wanted to stay alive. Well, for the next three or four days I did not venture anywhere near his locality. I told his sister what her idiot brother had done. She expressed her helplessness in the matter. The rumour spread through college that I had molested his sister. I was called in to the Principal's office and admonished for deliberately calling this upon myself by mixing with the local riffraff.

The Principal was a nice chap, who knew my family and also knew what a good boy I was. Although the girl's brother and her family were demanding my expulsion, the Principal said in that case he would also have to expel their daughter, and asked them to consider the scandal *that* would cause. Until the ruckus didn't blow over, I was walking about with a six-inch dagger strapped around my waist and a knuckle-duster in my pocket. A few months later, at a school picnic, the whole issue got sorted out and that brother who wanted to "Dree-eenk my bl-lood" shook my hand and said let's forget all about what happened. Mercifully, not a whiff of this scandal reached the ears of my mother who would have probably marched off to see the Principal and demand that both the girl and her brother be expelled for levelling such absurd accusations against a member of one of the finest families of Mussoorie.

Determined to shine in my Master's exams after the humiliating and dismal performance I had delivered during my B.A., I began putting in several hours of study each day well before the finals were to be held. I was always a *ratta-maar*[3] kind of a student, akin to a parrot who learns to rattle off a word or a phrase after it is continually repeated to it. I memorised the answers to questions set out in Guides and Keys, the short-cuts available to students to prepare for their exams.

I committed them to memory, word-for-word, without at times even bothering to understand the meaning of what I was memorising. The second trick I learnt for scoring high marks in exams was revealed by a freshman in the college. He told me to write the answers in a large, scrawling hand and fill up as many additional answer sheets as I could. On my asking how this would help, he said that the examiners looked for quantity rather than quality and judged a paper by its bulk – that is the number of additional answer sheets attached to the preliminary one.

---

3 Learning by rote.

Both the techniques worked in my favour. When the results were out, I had not only scored the highest marks but had also beaten the girl who was the teacher's pet and who had been expected to top the list that year. She went chalk-white on seeing the result and learning that I had pipped her to the post. More than anything else, I was relieved that I had not lost face again in front of my mother and had to some extent retrieved my honour. This piece of good news was considered worthy enough to be trunk-called that very night (The rates for trunk calls had halved after 9 pm) to my sisters in Mumbai. They also suggested that I be packed off to that city as soon as I had my mark sheet in hand. I demurred.

I approached my Principal, the same one who had saved me from being expelled, in his office a couple of days later and asked him to appoint me as a junior lecturer in the college. He cast his baleful, unblinking stone-eye at me that was much smaller than his functional eye and said, "Ee-yyungg man, don't be a prize fool, they will not let me hire a non-Garhwali. Besides, what will you earn here... peanuts, peanuts! Go to Bombay!"

"But what will I do in Bombay, Sir?" I pleaded with him. "I can't act, nor sing... I can't become an actor! And look how thinny-skinny I am!" Bombay to us meant only one thing and that was 'cinema'.

He squinted at me, viciously it now seemed, and pointing a quivering finger at the door, admonished, "GO! Before I call your mother and tell her that you will always remain a good-for-nothing!" To drive the knife deeper, he added with sly relish, "And, I will also tell her about the time I nearly had to expel you from college over that affair that almost brought shame to your family and my college. Go and do what your family is advising, Make something of your life there! There is nothing for you here!"

At the mention of that sordid incident, I flushed, blushed and broke out in a sweat. And fled!

Chapter 29

Leaving Home

Along the deserted platform, the train stood still.

Outside, the hills had begun to darken as dusk enveloped them in its diaphanous shroud.

It would be another hour before the Dehradun Express would pull out of the station. My mother, in her widow's whites, along with my friend Ganesh who had accompanied us from Mussoorie down to Dehradun, sat with me in the first class compartment.

Conversation had come to a dead halt. There was nothing left to say.

I urged my mother and Ganesh to leave as they had to return to Mussoorie. There was no point in their hanging around to see the train pull out. After some persuasion, they agreed it would be better if they left, so they could reach home before night fall.

I sat by the window and unspooled the silent movie of events that had brought me to this point in my journey. I wanted to get off the train and run after my mother, who would now be all alone for the next couple of months in Mussoorie before she could join me in Bombay. She had to stay back to wind up the house after which there would be no reason for her to stay on in Mussoorie. My father had passed away a couple of months earlier, my sisters were married and living in Bombay. They had insisted that I would fare better in that city and, above all, both my mother and I would be much better off staying close by.

The sing-song chant of *"Chai garam, chai garam,"*[1] by a strolling tea boy, rattling his makeshift wire-holder that held steaming glasses of tea, jerked me back to reality. A passenger got into the compartment and adjusted his luggage under the seat opposite mine.

A guard went by waving a green flag. The engine let out a shrill blast. The wheels made a jarring, grinding noise as they turned slowly on the rails. In the distance, the lights of Mussoorie had begun to glow and twinkle like fireflies in the night.

Swallowing a couple of lumps that rose in my throat, I craned my neck around to take one last glimpse. My eyes had misted over and the hills were a blur as they began receding into the distance.

Then, they were lost to me forever as the train turned a bend and chugged into the night...

---

[1] Hot tea, hot tea.

Thanks and Acknowledgements

My friend Quateel planted the seed for this book one evening, when after a long chat four years ago, he remarked: "Compared to most of us Shiv, you have had quite an eventful life. Why don't you put it all down?" Well, the seed took some time to take root. And then it started to sprout. So, my first thanks go out to him.

Then to my sisters, nephews and nieces who said the initial manuscript regaled them no end! And they weren't just being polite.

Heartfelt thanks go out to Ruskin Bond and Ganesh Saili, whom I have known for many years, and Bill Aitken, to pen their thoughts in the form of early reviews on my debut effort.

A very special word of thanks to Gautam Sachdeva for making sure this book sees the light of day.

Thanks to Priya Mehta for her conceptualisation and contemporary design for the book cover.

And above all, to the characters who populate its pages. If they had not crossed my path, this book would not have crossed yours!

I hope you enjoy reading it, if not as much as they did because some of them of course knew me personally, then just for the love of the Himalayan foothills and people everywhere who touch our lives in memorable ways. I am sure many have touched and helped shape your lives too.

We owe everyone who crosses our path, a debt of gratitude.

The author may be contacted on email:
shivds@gmail.com

For further details, contact:
India Impressions
(A Division of Yogi Impressions Books Pvt. Ltd.)
1711, Centre 1, World Trade Centre,
Cuffe Parade, Mumbai 400 005, India.
Telephone: (022) 61541500, 61541541

Also visit: www.indiaimpressions.in

Join us on Facebook:
www.facebook.com/indiaimpressions
www.facebook.com/yogiimpressions